The Lopsided Miracle

by

Emily E. Shipp

authorHOUSE

1663 Liberty Drive, Suite 200
Bloomington, Indiana 47403
(800) 839-8640
www.authorhouse.com

This book is a work of fiction. Places, events, and situations in this story are purely fictional and any resemblance to actual persons, living or dead, is coincidental.

© 2004 Emily E. Shipp
All Rights Reserved.

No part of this book may be reproduced, stored in a retrieval system, or transmitted by any means without the written permission of the author.

First published by AuthorHouse 05/19/04

ISBN: 1-4184-0216-8 (e)
ISBN: 1-4184-0215-X (sc)
ISBN: 1-4184-0214-1 (dj)

Library of Congress Control Number: 2004093389

Printed in the United States of America
Bloomington, Indiana

This book is printed on acid-free paper.

PART ONE

CHAPTER ONE

"Pass, please," the bus driver said in a rough voice. He was fat and had a moustache so thick Clem was sure there were things living in it. She rustled in her purse and brought out her bus pass. The bus driver looked at it, looked at Clem, and then grunted. Clem quickly put her bus pass away and bustled to the middle of the bus, where her best friend, Scarlett, was sitting, waiting for her.

"God, what is that bus driver *on*?" Scarlett asked Clem. "He's like mad at everybody!"

"I know," Clem replied. "But maybe he's just having a bad ..." All of a sudden, the bus left with a jerk, and Clem and Scarlett were pushed backwards.

"I hate this bus," Scarlett mumbled. She liked to complain.

Clem was usually the one to bring out the bright side. "Well, get used to it; you ride here a lot!" Clem said cheerfully. Scarlett looked at her with annoyance.

"Why and how can you be so cheerful today?" Scarlett asked.

Clem sighed and lay back in the black, old leather seat. "Today, my friend," Clem started, "is the beginning of the second season of *The Truth Told by Me*." Clem smiled and stared at the ceiling.

"Oh jeez, not that horrible show you're always raging about?" Scarlett asked.

"It is *not* a horrible show! It's great!" Clem protested.

"Oh, please. The only reason you like it is because that guy is on it. What's his name? Fred Mavis?"

"No! I *love* the show!" Clem piped. "And his name is Ben Clavis," she added quietly.

"Oops, my bad," Scarlett said sarcastically.

Emily E. Shipp

"What's got you eaten up? You don't usually care what I watch!" Clem said.

"Nothing," Scarlett said.

It didn't look like nothing.

"Come on, Scarlett, you can tell me anything; you know that," Clem comforted.

"I'll tell you later. This is your stop," Scarlett pointed out.

She was right. Kids were filing off the bus, and Clem hadn't noticed. Clem quickly put her backpack on her shoulder, took her metal lunchbox in her hand, and waved goodbye to Scarlett. She followed a group of other kids off the bus and then walked up into the rich neighborhood and onto her sunny driveway.

Clem opened the door to the usual scene. Her two-year-old identical twin brothers were playing somewhere off in the living room. Her eight-year-old identical triplet sisters were eating and joking in the kitchen. Her mother was reading a magazine on the white leather couch in the living room, supposedly watching the twins, Tommy and Travis.

"Mom, I'm home!" Clem shouted over the racket of a baby music-maker. Knowing that her mother hadn't heard her, Clem kicked off her shoes and put them in her spot in the hall closet. She raced upstairs and opened the door to her room to find that her TV had already been turned on. Her seventeen-year-old brother, Stephen, was sitting on the floor eating chips, watching it.

"Stephen!" Clem yelled. She dropped her backpack, walked over to him, picked up the remote, and turned the TV off.

Stephen looked at her with an angry expression. "Hello? I was watching that!" he protested.

"Hello? This is my room!" she pointed out impatiently.

"Yeah, but your TV is better than mine!" he said, standing up and making his tall, six-foot body its full length. Clem tried to look tall, but five foot five was not much compared to six foot.

"Get out," she said frostily. "I have to do my homework!"

The Lopsided Miracle

"Fine!" he yelled, picking up his bowl of Doritos. "I'll watch it in Mom's room!" He marched out as if he owned the place. She rolled her eyes and plopped down on her desk chair, wondering vaguely why she had a brother as stupid as her own. Looking over at her things, she realized that she hadn't put her lunchbox away. She groaned, really not wanting to go all the way back down to the kitchen.

The only horrible thing about having a huge house, she thought, heaving a sigh. It was true. The Greenly's *did* live in a large home. They had to. For every child to have his or her own room, they needed all the space. Grumpily, she got up and snatched the lunchbox from under her backpack, glaring at it as though it had feelings.

She reached the large staircase and slid down the banister, smiling like she always did when she repeated this childhood act. Once she reached the bottom, she ran into the kitchen where her three sisters were chatting carelessly. Only Bailey noticed she entered.

"Hi, Clem!" She laughed. Clem was something of a role model to Bailey. Clem didn't mind. She loved Bailey in a way that didn't apply to her other sisters.

"Hi, Bailey," Clem smiled. She walked over and put her lunchbox away by the microwave.

"What are you doing here, *Clementine*?" asked Beverly, who was prissy and fluffy and pink and knew Clem hated her full name.

"Well, what are you doing here, Beverly?" Clem mimicked in a high-pitched tone.

Beverly frowned. "Be quiet, Clementine," she threw out.

"Guys, will you please stop bickering?" Brooke, the straight-A student, pleaded.

"She started it," Beverly mumbled. Clem scowled at her. The trio all had short, brown bobs for hair, and they all had green eyes. Clem had brown hair and green eyes, too, but she had long, straight hair with curls at the bottom. The three were all the same height, practically the

Emily E. Shipp

same weight, and loved the same foods. Yet it was so easy to tell them apart.

Beverly, the eldest by fifteen seconds, loved everything pink and fluffy. Bailey, who was younger than Beverly but older than Brooke by ten seconds, only wore earth colors and never, ever in her life, wore a skirt or dress. She also liked nature and the stars and everything outside. Brooke was the smart one. She kept every molecule of her life organized.

Clem looked at the three eating licorice together, laughing joyfully. Even though they were so totally different, they were each other's best friends. Clem smiled and walked out, thinking about *her* best friend, Scarlett.

What was wrong? Why was she acting so strange and grouchy today?

I'll find out soon enough, Clem thought, making plans to call her.

As soon as she reached her own room, she flopped down in her desk chair once more and picked up her white phone, planning to dial Scarlett's phone number. The chilly blue glow of the numbers caught her eye and distracted her for a moment. She had just redone her room so that everything was sharp and icily modern. Sometimes she wished it were still pastel and childish, so that she would feel more at home there. Clem shook her head and wondered why she was thinking about her new room. Quickly, she dialed Scarlett's phone number. After four rings, Mrs. McIntyre picked up the phone.

"Hello?" she asked in an out-of-breath way.

"Hey, Mrs. McIntyre. Did I call at a bad time?" Clem asked.

"Oh, well, actually, it would have been better if you had called later," Mrs. McIntyre said.

Clem swallowed. "Oh, sorry, Mrs. McIntyre. Is Scarlett home?"

"Well, actually, she's gone visiting her fath … I mean …" She cut off quickly. "Um, she's not here at the moment, but I will tell her you

The Lopsided Miracle

called, Clem dear," Mrs. McIntyre said. She was a pet-name person: "Scarlett love," "Clem dear." As Clem thought about this, she wondered why Mrs. McIntyre seemed so eager to get off the phone.

"Okay, well, thanks anyway, Mrs. McIntyre," Clem said.

"Alright, Clem darling. Buh-bye." She hung up.

Clem hung up too, but did not take her eyes off the phone. What was that all about? Why did the normally calm Mrs. McIntyre seem so uptight and secretive? Clem decided not to think about it, because she looked at her clock and realized she had other things to worry about.

Oh! Clem thought. *It's four o'clock!* She leaned back in her chair, grabbed the remote, and flicked on the TV to the theme song music of *The Truth Told by Me.*

~

"Ha!" Jodie smiled and flicked her card onto the top of the pile of cards. "A two of spades! I win again!" She gathered up the cards in one hand and smiled at Ben.

"Shut up," he said. "You're just lucky. I'll get you one of these days."

"Oh, please," said Jodie. "Want to play again?"

"Yeah right. I can't stand the humiliation of being beaten by my younger sister again," he said.

"Oh, shut up. I'm only a year younger than you are, and I can whip the crap out of you if I want to," Jodie said, smiling her straight-teeth-under-braces smile. She put the cards back in the package and stood up.

"I'm going to practice lines with Mark. Want to come?" she asked.

Ben sighed. "No, thanks. If I look at my lines one more time, I'm going to start seeing in black and white," he said.

Jodie laughed. "Okay, fine by me." She left, popping an apple-flavored Jolly Rancher in her mouth on the way.

Emily E. Shipp

    Ben sat in his seat and watched his sister walk away. She was tall and thin and had long, blond hair, almost the same color as his. Her blue eyes and tan skin were pretty, and he had trouble convincing a lot of guys on the set that she wasn't interested. He laid his head back on the uncomfortable seat of the chair, but decided while he was relaxing that he might as well make himself useful. He stood up and walked past his sister's trailer where he could hear her fake screaming and Mark's voice.

    He walked into an office right beside the makeup area. His eyes looked through the little window of the door where his agent, a short, scrawny man with a bright purple suit coat on, was chattering into a phone, his tie flopping over the phone line. Ben pushed the door open.

    "Yes, I understand, Mrs. Queenly, but I don't necessarily think it is a good idea. It would be much too risky … No, Mrs. Queenly … Yes, Mrs. Queenly." The agent turned around and jumped back when he saw Ben's face.

    "Uh, uh … M … Mrs. Queenly, I must go. I will take your thought into consideration." He clutched the phone tightly while hanging up in an unusually bottled manner. He stared at Ben.

    "What do you want?" Mr. Carton asked reluctantly.

    "Um, sorry, Joe," Ben said, raising an eyebrow.

    Mr. Carton sighed. "I'm sorry, Ben, but there is just this issue with the boss." He looked up quickly and then decided to say something else. "But you don't need to know about that. What did you need?" he asked.

    I wonder what he's not telling me, Ben thought, but decided not to bring it up. "I wanted to know if I had any mail today," he asked, walking over to his mail slot on the right wall. He checked in the space. There were three letters there. "Three. Yesterday, I had five," he said egotistically.

The Lopsided Miracle

"Well, settle with what you have," Mr. Carton said, as if Ben had complained about not having enough food when there was a feast in front of him. He cleared his throat and walked out of the office.

Ben looked down at his letters. One of them was a pink envelope that smelled strongly of perfume. He just knew there would be a lip print on the back. He looked at the next letter—a letter with the return name and address printed carefully in the top corner. Ben snorted. Then he looked at the last one. He recognized it right away. The girl who wrote it, Clem Greenly, had been writing him almost every week for the past six months. Her envelope was a plain, white envelope with loopy handwriting in the center, spelling out his name. The ink was green and there were smiley stickers littering the front. He stared at the letter, wondering what mushy words lay inside. Clutching the letters in his hands, he walked back out of the office and wandered to Jodie's trailer to read them.

Reaching the trailer, he opened the door to see that Ryan Matthews, another guy from the show, had joined Jodie and Mark.

"Good sir, please do not leave me. I do not know what I would do if I reached the king and told him his guest did not want to see him—" said Jodie, playing Felicity.

"What the heck?" Mark said, reading off his lines, "Where am I?"

"Good, kind sir. You are at King Rogerson's castle. He was awaiting the guest of honor. I can only assume that is you?"

"Uh ... yeah, I guess. Felicity, what's going on?"

"Felicity? How do you know my name?" Jodie said.

"Stop! Take it from the top!" Ben's voice cut through the dramatic scene in which Mark's character, John, was taken into the past.

"Ben! Come on! I'm trying to be a princess in distress!" Jodie said.

"Did you know that you guys were rhyming, like, every sentence?" Ryan asked.

Emily E. Shipp

Jodie looked at him and hit the top of his head with the script. "Put a sock in it! You're ruining the mood," said Jodie. "Come on, Ben, if you're going to listen, then sit down before I lose character."

"Nah, I'm not going to listen. I'm reading fan mail," he said, waving his letters around.

"Well, whatever," Mark said. "Just make sure you're here for the kissing scene." He waggled his eyebrows. Jodie hit the top of his head, too.

"Yeah, go," Ben told them. He made his way into a small room at the end of the trailer and closed the door. Looking briefly at the letters, he decided that he would read Clem's first. He tore open the envelope and brought out the letter, reading the cursive handwriting. *Dear Ben …*

CHAPTER TWO

"Mom, can I go over to Scarlett's?" Clem asked. She had just finished watching the new episode of *The Truth Told by Me*. She had loved all the characters' parts and had practically melted when she saw Ben on the screen. She had received a message on her answering machine from Mrs. McIntyre that Scarlett returned home.

"Excuse me, young lady, but you just got home! What about dinner?" Mrs. Greenly said.

"Mom, I don't want any dinner! If I'm hungry, I'll ... I'll just eat something at Scarlett's," Clem said, putting on her sweater and passing the Christmas tree on the way to the door.

"Clem, don't you want to wait until your father gets home?" she tried once more.

"No, Mom!" she said, opening the front door. "Tell him I said hello." She closed the door behind her.

In South Carolina, there wasn't much of a winter. It was still hot outside and it *never* snowed. Clem wished that there was some excuse to get out of school and have a snow day, but of course, there never, ever was.

She hopped on her bike and pushed herself out of the driveway and down the road. Scarlett's street was two streets over from Clem's and the convenience of it was fabulous—especially now that Clem needed to talk to Scarlett, and Scarlett obviously needed to talk to Clem.

The sprinklers were on by the time Clem rode into Scarlett's driveway. She had to fight her way through, making sure she didn't get wet, into Scarlett's garage where she always parked her bike.

Two cars were there, like always. There was Scarlett's mother's Mustang and Scarlett's father's Jeep Grand Cherokee. Clem parked her

Emily E. Shipp

deep blue bike next to Scarlett's old hula-hoops and a scooter that she hardly ever used anymore. Making her way toward the door, she heard voices coming from the kitchen.

"Marty, I swear I will not take any more of this! You are being ridiculous."

"Me, Mina? It's all you! It's always about you!"

"Marty, I want you out of my house right now!" Mrs. McIntyre screamed.

"Fine! And see if I ever come back!" Mr. McIntyre yelled back in his booming, echoing voice. Clem could hear him blast open the door to the garage. Clem, confused and scared, hurriedly scrambled behind a tool bench that Mr. McIntyre always used. She heard the door slam shut.

"I swear to Betsy that when that woman is logical, it will be the end of the world!" Mr. McIntyre said to himself. All of a sudden, Clem saw his feet stop on the concrete floor of the garage and turn toward Clem's hiding spot. Clem caught her breath. If she were caught lurking around in the McIntyre's garage, it would be the end of their trust forever. If she had just casually walked in, pretending not to hear them, then she would have had an excuse for waiting in the garage. But this? They would automatically assume she was eavesdropping.

Clem prayed with all her might as his shoes drew nearer. Then, almost a foot away from her, he stopped.

Please, please, please! Clem begged silently. Then, to her great relief, she heard him pick up a toolbox from on top of the bench and march back to his car. He opened the door and then revved up the engine. She heard his car door slam and his wheels roll out of the garage, onto the driveway and out onto the road, passing the cheery, perfect houses on the way to the main street. Clem sighed and got up, her sneakers squeaking on the floor. She walked to the door and knocked as normally as she could. She felt Mrs. McIntyre coming

The Lopsided Miracle

towards the door. She had started talking before she reached the door and flung it open.

"Go away you mangy scum. Oh!" She saw Clem standing innocently in front of her. Mrs. McIntyre blushed and wiped wisps of red hair behind her ears. "I'm sorry, Clem. This really isn't a good time. Can you come back later?" she asked, looking as though she were on the verge of tears.

"Actually, can you just send Scarlett out? I really need to talk to her," Clem said. Mrs. McIntyre managed to nod as she let the door close on Clem.

"Scarlett, honey? Clem's here." Clem heard Mrs. McIntyre call for Scarlett. There was muffled yelling from the daughter, but after a few words from her mother, Scarlett came down the steps and opened the garage door.

Clem did a quick survey of her friend. If Mrs. McIntyre looked bad, it was nothing compared with how Scarlett looked. Her face was pale and wan, and her red hair was not up in its usual ponytail, but in front of her ears and eyes. Although her eyes were covered up with a large amount of hair, Clem could still see very clearly that they were red, puffy, and irritated.

"I ...I ..." but Scarlett couldn't say anything. Clem led her speechless friend out of the garage, down the road, and into a nearby park where carolers' voices could be heard in the distance. They sat down on a bench that was dry and uncomfortable, but Clem didn't think Scarlett could stand for one more second.

Scarlett looked at Clem for a long time, studying her. Then Scarlett flung herself into Clem's arms and burst into tears.

"Oh, Clem! Clem, it's horrible! It's my parents! They were so happy together and now ..." She couldn't go on. Her voice was covered with a coat of sobs. Immediately, Clem enveloped Scarlett in a friendly embrace.

Emily E. Shipp

"Shhh ... It's okay ... It's going to be okay ..." Clem soothed. Scarlett just continued to weep into Clem's sweater.

For about five long minutes, Scarlett just lay down and cried while Clem whispered comforting words and patted Scarlett's head as though she was a long-lost puppy. But then, suddenly and without warning, Scarlett sat up and let out a large hiccup.

"I'm sorry, Scarlett," Clem said. "What happened?"

Scarlett wiped her eyes with her sleeve, but it didn't help much. "My parents have ... *hiccup* ... been going through fights about money ... *hiccup* ... and they ... and they are ..." and before she could even say it, she was plunging into fresh tears again. Instead of reaching for Clem, she brought her legs up to her face and hid her tears in the depths of her jeans.

"Are they getting a divorce?" Clem asked. At that word, Scarlett bawled like a baby. "Look, Scarlett, I'm sorry. I'm really sorry, and you know what? I know your parents are, too, but you have to buck up! Remember what you told me when my parrot died? Remember?" Scarlett looked up and shook her head. "You told me to be brave. You told me that in any situation, you have to look on the bright side; make the best of it! Now ... now look at you!" Clem gestured to Scarlett's current looks.

Scarlett wiped her nose on the cuff of her sweatshirt. "I can't help it. Besides, you were just losing a parrot. I'm losing both my parents!" she cried.

"No you're not!" Clem said. "You're keeping them both! And this way, they'll be even happier than before, even with money problems."

"I don't understand why they are having money problems! I mean, my dad's a lawyer and my mom is a *songwriter* for a popular *singer*, for goodness sake, bringing in *thousands* of dollars a year! A *songwriter*, Clem! I think it's just that my dad doesn't like her anymore and the money is a big cover up," she heaved. Clem sighed.

The Lopsided Miracle

"Well, whatever it is, I think they'll both be happier this way. If not, then they wouldn't be getting a divorce," Clem said. She could see Scarlett trying not to cringe.

"That's not the way it should be, though. They should be happy *together* ... not apart!" Scarlett wailed. Clem looked at her. She knew she had to help her friend get out of all this despair, but how?

Clem touched her friend's shoulder and smiled softly. "Listen, I know you're going through a hard time. I'm really glad you told me. Now, I'm going to find some way to get you to be happy again or get you spiritually away from all of this, okay?" Clem said in a stubborn, but helpful way.

Scarlett looked up at Clem. "Well, thanks, but I think this is just one of those things that I have to do alone," she said dully.

"No! It is not! I'm going to help you as much as I can, got it?" Clem said.

Scarlett just stared, but then finally sighed. "Fine, but you won't have much luck."

"Not by myself, no," Clem said.

Scarlett widened her eyes. "No! No, no, no, no, no!" Scarlett said, shaking her hands in front of her, her sadness turning into defensiveness. "I'm not going to become one of those kids who becomes... *mental* because of divorce!"

"Yes, you are. It will help you," Clem said.

"No, it won't. Now if you'll excuse me, I have to go home and sob some more," she said with a tear rolling down her cheek.

"You are making this whole situation worse than it already is," Clem said.

Scarlett jerked her head up and glared at Clem. "Well, I'm so sorry I'm not saying, 'Yep, I'm glad my parents are divorcing'!" she yelled, shooting up off the bench and clutching her fists.

"Sorry, Scarlett, I'm just trying to help," Clem said.

Emily E. Shipp

Scarlett let out a growl. "That's what my parents said! Now look what happened to them!" Scarlett said. She started crying again and ran off in the direction of her house.

"Scarlett! Scarlett, wait!" Clem got up and called after Scarlett. Clem dropped her hands down to her sides reluctantly and slouched.

Well, that went well, she thought. Looking at the ground in despair, she saw an acorn. She bent over and picked it up, looking at its round shape and cap-like head.

I remember when we used to play with these, Clem thought, *and made them into little people.* She sighed.

"Acorn, you do not know how lucky you are to be an inanimate object."

~

Dinner was always a discussion time for the Clavises. Mr. and Mrs. Clavis would talk about their days at work while Ben and Jodie would rant about what was wrong with their lives. Tonight seemed like it would be a nice, normal night for the Clavises.

Or so Ben thought.

He came downstairs to a dinner of fried chicken, mashed potatoes, rolls, green beans, cornbread, and milk. He was beginning to like his mother's new delight in country cooking. He smiled at his mother. His mother was a beautiful, tall, lean person who looked like she wore makeup all the time. She was wearing a white blouse and a short, white-and-black checkered skirt today.

"Ben! There you are! Do you know what your sister is doing?" she asked, putting a glass of milk by a plate.

"Mom, do I *ever* know what Jodie is doing?" Ben asked. Mrs. Clavis gave him a look. "Okay! Sorry. I'll go get her," he said, shoving his hands in his pockets. Clapping his feet against the carpeted staircase, he could hear his sister in her room, singing to a tune that Ben's band had written. Mark Olshire and Ryan Matthews from *The Truth Told by*

The Lopsided Miracle

Me were also in the band. He knocked on the door. She opened it and looked at him in an annoyed fashion.

"What?" she asked.

"Dinner," he grumbled.

"Oh," she said. They had this conversation every night, but somehow, they never got tired of it. Jodie followed him down the steps and into the kitchen. They sat down in their regular places, right next to each other.

Jodie and Ben were not like other brothers and sisters. They fought, of course, but they shared a special bond that most other brothers and sisters did not share. They were on a TV show together, they sat next to each other at dinner, and they talked to each other about their feelings if something was wrong. They weren't exactly friends, but they were as close as friends can get when they happen to be siblings.

Mr. Clavis walked in just then, briefcase in one hand and suit coat in the other. "Hello, everyone," he said, hanging up his coat and kicking off his shoes. He kissed the top of Jodie's head. "How is my angel muffin?"

Jodie cringed. She found this name very annoying. "There is no one here named angel muffin, Dad," she said through clenched teeth.

He laughed. "I know. Just wanted to get a rise out of you," he said. He gave Ben a happy smile and then set off to put his briefcase away. Jodie turned to Ben.

"Well, Dad's acting normal," she said. Ben laughed, and their mother came in the room once more.

"I thought I heard Dad come in," she said.

"He did," Ben told her. "He's putting his briefcase away."

"Can we please eat?" Jodie asked impatiently.

"Jodie! Of course not! Not until your dad gets back to the table," she said, placing a slice of cornbread on Jodie's plate. Jodie rolled her eyes.

Emily E. Shipp

"How stupid a rule is that?" she mumbled. Mrs. Clavis chose to ignore it. "Thanks, Mom, but when Dad gets back here, we'll have all died of starvation," Jodie pointed out.

Mrs. Clavis sighed. "All right, fine. But say grace before you eat," she said. Jodie and Ben closed their eyes and prayed a silent prayer, finishing at almost the exactly same time. Jodie dug into her mashed potatoes while Ben picked at his green beans.

"I think these things are alive," Ben observed.

Jodie hit his head with her fork. "You're such a dork," she said.

About fifteen minutes later, the whole family was seated and ready to eat together. The parents finished saying their prayers, and then they all dove into conversation.

"Well everyone, I just want you all to know that I passed my algebra test today after long, hard, laboring hours of studying. It finally paid off!" Jodie bragged.

"Good, good," Mrs. Clavis said. "I'm so happy to know that this show isn't taking you away from your studies," she logically put in.

"Mom. It never did," Jodie said, wearing a "duh" face.

"I know, but there is a first for everything," Mrs. Clavis said.

"Mom!"

"Excuse me!" Mr. Clavis interrupted. "I have had a long, hard day at the office with lots of other arguments, and I will not tolerate another one now, especially over something that doesn't need arguing over."

"Dad!"

"Ah," he said, holding up a finger to keep Jodie quiet. She slouched back in her chair and fiddled with her fork in her food, mumbling.

"Well, guys, guess who called today?" Mrs. Clavis asked.

"Who?" Ben asked, not really caring. He wanted the fight between his sister and his father to go on longer.

"Mrs. Queenly," she said. Jodie, who hated Mrs. Queenly, snorted in her milk.

The Lopsided Miracle

"Oh," Ben said, not understanding what was so interesting. Ben looked at his mother. Was it just him, or was his mother looking extremely uncomfortable?

"She said she was coming by around seven," Mrs. Clavis informed them.

"What?" both teens said at once.

Even Mr. Clavis almost dropped his napkin. "Excuse me?" He looked his wife in the eye and lowered his voice. "Since when does that witch make house calls?" he asked in a loud whisper.

Jodie smiled. "You tell her, Dad!"

Mrs. Clavis gave him a *what-kind-of-example-are-you-setting-for-the-kids* look.

"Sorry," he muttered. "Kids, never say that," he said. Jodie and Ben looked at each other with a *parents* look.

"Yes, Mrs. Queenly said she had something very important to talk about with Jodie and Ben," she said, gesturing to the two youths.

"Oh great," Jodie said. "Just what I need. I've already got pimples; the last thing I need is a wart."

"Jodie!" Mrs. Clavis said. "Quit it. I've had enough smart-mouth from you to last a lifetime. Just go upstairs and make yourself appropriate for your boss." She made sure she added emphasis to "your boss." Jodie let out a grunt and marched upstairs, not believing that her mother was being so strict.

"Mom, why couldn't you just tell her that we're busy or something?" Ben asked.

"Ben, look, I don't ... I mean, I don't necessarily have the biggest liking for her either ... But she sounded like she really wanted to talk to you two, so please be nice, won't you?" Mrs. Clavis said.

Ben looked at them both, sighed, and then stared at his food. *I wish I were mashed potatoes,* he thought sullenly, *because all their troubles are over within a chew and a swallow.* He took his napkin away from his lap.

Emily E. Shipp

"Fine," he said.

There were very good reasons why the majority of the Clavises hated Mrs. Queenly. For one, she was bossy and loved to order people around like they were her slaves. Another reason they did not like her was because she was a horrible conversationalist. She always made people uncomfortable and nervous when they were trying to think of something to say. But the biggest reason they didn't like her was because she was very cold-hearted and had no sympathy at all. She was simply greedy. Neither of the Clavis children understood how she could create a show as creative as *The Truth Told by Me*. Just by looking at her, most people would think she was completely left-brained.

So at 6:55, all of the Clavises were scurrying around, trying to prepare everything. The living room had not a speck of dust in it, everything was polished, (including Jodie and Ben), and Mrs. Clavis had made hors d'oeuvres. Even though they didn't really like Mrs. Queenly, they needed to make a good impression on her.

Ben was settled on the couch, his socked feet up, reading *Sports Illustrated* while his mom was fussing over fried shrimp.

"Well, what do you think, Ben? Is it too much?" she asked, holding out the silver plate filled with rings of shrimp and lettuce.

Ben raised an eyebrow at his mother. "Are you sure you want me to answer that?" he asked.

She lifted the plate away from him in a flounce. "Well, I hope you like shrimp, because this is what we're having," she said. All of a sudden, the doorbell rang and she almost dropped the plate. She quickly set it down on the coffee table.

"Coming!" she yelled. "Okay, Ben, we have the hors d'oeuvres, you ... where's your sister?" The doorbell rang again. "Gosh, that woman has no patience. Ben, go find your sister," she said, bustling to the door in her jeans and beige sweater. Ben went upstairs in his own jeans and T-shirt, looking for Jodie and hoping she was somewhere far off so that

The Lopsided Miracle

he could spend the whole visit looking for her instead of having to sit through stiff conversation with Mrs. Queenly.

No such luck.

As soon as he reached the top step, Jodie came out of her room in jeans and a red-and-white-checkered midriff top with puffed sleeves. Her hair was flipped out like always, and the only thing that wasn't pretty about her was the expression on her face. She looked as if she had just swallowed a roach.

"Is Mrs. Queenly here?" she asked tightly.

"If she wasn't, why would Mom be serving fried shrimp with lettuce and little cherry tomatoes?" Ben asked.

"Great," Jodie said, closing her door. "I heard she's into the peasant look on teenagers, or at least the ones she likes anyway," she added quickly. "So I'm trying to be as peasanty as I can to avoid more criticism about how I act," she said, leading the way down the steps. When they reached the bottom, they both stared at exactly what they were expecting.

Mrs. Queenly was there with her hands straight down to her sides and posture so rigid it seemed as though she had a board up her back. She was wearing sharp, navy, spiked heels with invisible hose and a white blouse tucked into a navy skirt and covered up by a navy suit coat with so much shoulder padding that if she shrugged her shoulders, Ben thought, she would reach the moon. She had her raven-black hair up in a tight bun and her brown eyes were like a hawk's. Ben had a queasy feeling she was going to bring out a knife, but instead she turned to Ben and Jodie and smiled her tight smile.

"Good evening, children." Ben cringed. He hated it when she called them children.

"Hey, Mrs. Queenly. Would you like to come into the living room? We have freshly made shrimp," Jodie said, sounding much more relaxed than she probably felt.

Emily E. Shipp

Mrs. Queenly's smile faded. "I hate shrimp," she said and walked into the living room. "And besides that, I am here strictly for business matters." She sat down on the maroon leather couch without slumping a bit.

"Well, Mrs. Queenly, may I ask what that business would be?" Mrs. Clavis said.

Mrs. Queenly looked Mrs. Clavis up and down as if she were a slug. "Excuse me, but I need to talk to Ben and Jodie *alone*," she said. She then pointed to the shrimp as if she had just smelled a skunk. "And take that wretched shrimp with you. I am allergic to that nasty smelling gunk."

Mrs. Clavis looked offended, but then she glared and smirked. "You know, Mrs. Queenly, why don't I take your coat, too?" she asked.

Mrs. Queenly stood up. "Actually, that would be nice," she said, taking off her coat. She carelessly threw her coat at Mrs. Clavis who caught it in her face. Mrs. Clavis jerked the coat away from her face and as calmly as she could, walked out of the room. Mrs. Queenly, who had no idea that she had just completely offended Ben and Jodie's mother, sat back down in her stiff position and stared at the two other curious souls in the room.

"Now, I don't want any poor sports when I tell you my idea. I have a feeling you'll like it just fine," she said. Ben and Jodie exchanged a glance. Mrs. Queenly kept going. "Anyway, as you two might have noticed, you are losing publicity fast." She obviously felt the need to get up, so she did. Mrs. Queenly's pacing made Ben feel sick. "So, last night, as I was thinking of a way to make *The Truth Told by Me* and its actors the biggest and the best, I received a phone call from my sister."

There are two Mrs. Queenly's? Oh, man, Ben thought.

"She was talking about how she was discussing an exchange program with the child she tutors in math, and then I was struck by an idea!" Her eyes bore into Ben's, and he felt the familiar uncomfortableness that he always felt around Mrs. Queenly.

The Lopsided Miracle

"Now," she said, sitting back down on the couch and slapping her hand on the table as if her palm was a whip, "without beating around the bush, I want to ask you two something. What could be more news-friendly than having a contest where two young actors take in a random fan and treat them to their humble home and lives? It would make us rich! The contest entries would be overflowing! We would be the most …"

"What?" Jodie yelled. "Whoa, whoa, back up a second! You're asking us to take in an exchange student just to have more publicity?" she asked. Ben would have said something, but he was completely tongue-tied. What was this woman thinking?

"What if we accidentally take in a robber? Or some *sick-minded* fan?" Jodie went on.

"Of course we have stats on the person we choose. We will, anyway. We will also have parent forms and everything else so the whole thing will be perfectly safe."

"Yeah, but it's not only that! Where will they stay? Where will they go to school?" Jodie asked.

"They will stay in the guest bedroom, of course, and they will go to your school," Mrs. Queenly said.

"No," Jodie said. "No! I won't have it," she said, bouncing up.

"You will, too!" Mrs. Queenly growled. Jodie didn't look a bit afraid, although Ben would have been.

"I will not! You cannot command me to do anything!" Jodie said, clenching her fists.

"I can, too. What if I told you that if you agreed, you would get paid double the price I pay you to be on the show?" she asked.

Jodie, who was about to throw a punch, lowered her fists and widened her eyes. "Double?" she asked dumbfounded.

"Yes, double," Mrs. Queenly repeated.

Ben sprung to speak. "Well, what about me?" he asked.

Emily E. Shipp

    Mrs. Queenly shot him a look. "You will, too. Just calm down!" she commanded. Ben obeyed. "Just think about it, you two! You'll meet a new person and get paid extra and all you will have to do is be welcoming hosts." She looked at them.

    "I don't know," Ben whispered. "It would be such a huge change."

    Mrs. Queenly looked at her watch. "Well, while you two think about it, I have an appointment with Mr. Carton." She stood up and looked both of them up and down. "Think about what I said. You have until Friday to think about it and make a decision. I'm sorry it will have to be a quick decision, but the deadline for all the forms is very soon." Then, without looking the slightest bit sorry, she turned on her heels and walked out of the room. Ben looked at Jodie.

    "I don't know, Jo," he said.

    "Well, neither do I. I mean it's not exactly a quick decision question when you ask if we want some random fan to come live with us," Jodie replied. Ben looked at the floor and then, before he could say something else, he had to jump up because he heard a shrill scream from the foyer. Jodie scrambled up, too.

    "What is that?" she asked. Ben didn't have time to answer They both ran to the foyer where they saw Mrs. Queenly, her face pale and angry, with her hands over her gaping mouth. Mrs. Clavis also came rushing in.

    "What is it? Oh!" she said, as she saw what was wrong. It was Mrs. Queenly's coat, covered in cocktail sauce. "Oh, Mrs. Queenly, I'm so sorry! I meant to tell you, when I was walking back to the kitchen, the shrimp plate slipped and ... "

    "Mrs. Clavis! I can't believe you would be so clumsy! This is a *$3,000* coat!" she cried. Mrs. Clavis tried to speak again, but before she could say a word, Mrs. Queenly had snatched up the filthy coat and marched out the door, cursing under her breath.

The Lopsided Miracle

As soon as the door closed, Jodie burst out laughing and ran into the living room to calm herself. Ben looked after her and then looked at his mother with an amused smile on his face.

"You didn't *accidentally* spill that cocktail sauce, did you, Mom?" he asked.

Mrs. Clavis glanced at him. She patted his shoulder and leaned into him. "Just don't tell your father," she said.

CHAPTER THREE

Clem was sitting in the library, looking at her homework as if expecting it to do tricks. She was not really paying attention to her sophomore algebra. She had been racking her brain all day over what she could possibly do to help Scarlett.

She thought of signing Scarlett up for therapy, but Clem knew Scarlett would never hear of it. She thought of asking the teachers to give up Scarlett's time in class so that she could see the guidance counselor, but she knew Scarlett thought the guidance counselor was deranged and smelled like dog saliva. She also thought of signing her up for a help group with kids her own age, but that was just out of the question, because she knew perfectly well that Scarlett would want her to go too, and Clem would never be caught dead in one of those help groups. Clem had thought of taking her own dad and Scarlett out on a camping trip for the weekend to calm Scarlett's nerves, but figured that would be stupid because all the fatherly love would make Scarlett sick for her own father. She thought of just inviting her for a sleepover, but that would remind her of old times, and that would make her sad.

Clem was completely out of ideas, as well as completely clueless about how to do her math assignment. She so badly wanted Scarlett to cheer up, but how? How would Scarlett ever cheer up again if her parents were separated?

Clem rested her chin on her hand and stared into the distance. Helping friends was tiring!

She was about to drift off to sleep when she felt a tap on her shoulder. She looked up with an exhausted expression on her face but perked up as soon as she saw who it was.

"Scarlett! What are you doing here? I thought you went home already!" Clem exclaimed.

Emily E. Shipp

Scarlett blushed at Clem's gesture to sit down. "Sorry, but I actually don't have any time to stay right now. I just came over to tell you to come over to my house at around 7:30. You will come, right?" Scarlett asked.

Clem was slightly dumbfounded at Scarlett's appearance, not to mention her request. A few days ago, Scarlett was raggedy and distressed. Now, she was freshly showered and had on what looked suspiciously like new clothes. The change was amazing.

"Uh ..." Clem shook away all her thoughts. "What?"

"I asked if you would come over to my house around 7:00 ..."

"No, no ... that's not what I mean." Clem looked at her math book and closed the front cover. "I mean, a couple of days ago, you were really mad at me, now you want me to come over. You're really confusing me."

"I'm sorry," Scarlett said, and she sounded it, too. She sat down with her bottom slightly perched on the seat next to Clem and rested her hand on Clem's arm. "Please! This is really important! *Pretty please!* With a cherry on top! Ice cream in the middle! Gummy Bears and chocolate chips ..."

"Blandishment is a very stupid way to talk me into something, Scarlett," Clem said, raising an eyebrow. Scarlett sighed, clearly looking disappointed. After a couple of seconds of Scarlett's head drooping like a limp noodle, Clem finally gave in, throwing her hands up in the air with defeat. "Okay, okay. I'll go," Clem said.

Scarlett's head flew up as she smiled like she had been given two million dollars. "Oh, thank you so much, Clem!" Scarlett said, hugging Clem so tightly she thought she was going to choke. "You'll be glad!" With that, she galloped out of the library as fast as a horse in a derby.

Clem grunted and started to pack up all of her things. Scarlett looked and sounded as good as new, so at least that burden was taken off Clem's shoulders, but the thing Clem wanted to know was *what* had caused this miraculous change in Scarlett? If Scarlett's own best friend

The Lopsided Miracle

could hardly help, then what could? Clem thought about this as she left the library, passing a punk in ripped jeans and a leather jacket.

She walked down the steps and into the fresh winter air, breathing it in deeply. She walked slowly down the school steps and started towards home.

What could it be? the little voice in her head asked. *What is it that is so important to Scarlett? Why does she want you to know about it?*

The questions lingered. They lingered throughout homework, they lingered throughout Beverly's endless tales about the day's pointless events, and they even almost distracted her from *The Truth Told by Me*.

Almost.

She couldn't wait until after dinner so she could go, but everyone seemed to be asking her questions that required essay-long answers.

"So, how was school today?" asked her father.

"Fine," she said.

"Oh, come on. Nothing can be just 'fine,'" he said. Clem had to go into detail about her day, and then listen to everyone else's boring details about their own personal lives.

So when Clem was fifteen minutes late getting to Scarlett's, she had a perfectly good excuse.

Scarlett swung open the door and grinned.

"Finally! I thought you'd never get here!" Scarlett said, opening the door wider.

"I'm sorry. My dad was in a 'let's talk' mood," Clem said, stepping inside from the slightly chilly weather. Clem shut the door.

"Come on, let's go to my room," Scarlett suggested eagerly. Clem shrugged and hid her hands in the depths of her jacket pockets as she followed Scarlett, who was moving at a slow sprint. Clem was tired of following her before they even reached the stairs.

"Jesus, Scarlett! Slow down!" Clem said, running out of breath on the last steps going upstairs.

Emily E. Shipp

"I'm sorry; I just really want you to see this!" Scarlett said, skidding into her room. Clem skidded in behind her.

"What in the world is so important?" Clem asked, taking her hands out of her pockets. She plopped herself onto a bright yellow beanbag chair as Scarlett rustled through a bunch of papers in her desk.

"Ah-ha!" she said, holding up a variety of colored papers, mostly white and blue.

Clem was sick of asking the question. "*What*? Are you ever going to tell me?" Clem wondered in a frustrated way.

"Okay, okay; I'm sorry. I'll tell you right now," she said, leaning backward on the desk, papers still in hand. They weren't facing Clem's way, or else she would have just read them then and there.

"All, right," Scarlett started, "You remember how you told me to start looking for a way to cheer myself up?"

Clem frowned. "Yeah, and remember how you ditched me?" she replied sourly.

"Hey! Would you please stop that? My parents are getting a divorce; you can't expect me to be as happy as a horse!" Scarlett blurted. She'd obviously wanted to say that for days, and it obviously still pained her to say the word "divorce."

"Okay, fine. I'll drop it if you'll just get to the point," Clem said.

Scarlett flicked the papers up. "Fine! It's a deal." She looked at the papers and then looked up at Clem again. "Well the thing is, I was really sick of everything that day. I mean, I just wanted to get away … and that's when it hit me … I *did* have to get away! See, I found a brochure lying on the ground near the school where someone had dropped it, and once I started looking at it, I got excited because I had found the answer to all my problems!" she rushed to say.

Clem raised an eyebrow. "Wow. I bet it's really great, then?"

Scarlett paid no attention to the large hint of sarcasm in this comment. "Oh, it is! Anyway, I went to the principal, and she talked to my parents, and I talked to my parents, and my parents signed the forms

The Lopsided Miracle

and now ..." She took a deep breath. "I'm part of a foreign exchange program."

There was a big silence in the room for about six seconds. Then Clem spoke.

"What?" she asked.

"Yeah!" Scarlett smiled. "Isn't it great? I'm part of a foreign exchange program where I get to travel to a different country and everything! It's going to be great! I'm going to just take a break from everything; I can get away without my parents! I mean what better solution is there?" she asked.

Clem shook her head. "Whoa! What? I ... I mean, you're just going to ... leave?" She had to choke out the last word.

Scarlett frowned. "Well ... aren't you happy for me?" she asked.

Clem sputtered. "Well, yeah, but no, I mean ... yeah, but what about ... I mean..." All her words were lost, and Scarlett looked hurt.

"Clem ... I thought you would be happy for me," she said.

Clem sighed and put her forehead on her hands. Then she looked back up. "No, it's not that. I am happy for you, Scarlett ... but what am I supposed to do without my best friend here?" she asked. "I'll miss you way too much."

There was another big silence, and then Scarlett began to talk uneasily. "Well ... you could always ... come with me."

All of a sudden, Clem's head jerked up and the expression on her face was massive surprise. She began to shake her head wildly. "No! No, no, no! There is no *way!* No possible way! Nuh-uh, wrong number, no way, I am *not* doing it. Mm-mm," she declared.

Scarlett sagged. "Uh! Clem!"

"That's the reason you brought me over here, isn't it?" Clem asked. "Because you wanted to see if I'd fall into your little trap!"

Scarlett opened and closed her mouth several times before she finally said, "Well ... kind of ..."

Emily E. Shipp

Clem rolled her eyes. "Scarlett, what were you thinking? Did you really think I was going to sign up for a *travel* program? You know I hate travel! I despise it," she said.

Scarlett furrowed her brow. "Well, why? What is so bad about traveling to a new place, meeting new people, learning a new culture? What is so bad about that?"

"Well ... I don't know ..." Clem was losing steam.

"Well what? Tell me, Clem. And tell me the truth: What if it was for my sake? What if it was for the sake of your best friend?" Scarlett asked.

Clem was about to speak, but then she quickly shut her mouth. Why didn't she want to travel? Why was she so afraid of going to a new place? Truthfully, Clem didn't know. Maybe she was presented with the idea too quickly; maybe in other circumstances she would have liked to try it.

"I ... I ..." Clem couldn't answer. She was so wrapped up in her thoughts and questions that she hardly noticed Scarlett giving her the papers about the travel exchange program.

"Well, if you do want to stick by my side while I do this, then here are the forms. You have to sign up by Friday, though."

Clem shook her head to relieve herself from the hard pondering. "Yeah, okay," she said. She started to leave, but Scarlett grabbed her arm.

"Oh, and Clem?"

Clem turned around. "What?"

"Just ... just think about what I said." The look in her eyes was so pitiful that Clem thought she was about to break down crying again, like the day in the park, "Please, Clem. Just think about it."

That night, even though she was in her most comfortable pajamas in her newly washed sheets and her head was lying on a feather-down pillow (she thought a more comfortable pillow would help her sleep),

The Lopsided Miracle

Clem Greenly was very uncomfortable. She tossed and turned like a salad all night long, thinking about nothing but the foreign exchange program. Scarlett's voice echoed in her head is if she were in a hollow cave. *Please, Clem. Just think about it.* Well, Scarlett had gotten her wish. Now there was nothing else Clem could think about.

Of course, there were pros and cons to either decision. If she were insane enough to want to travel to a different country on such short notice, then yes, she would be able to meet new people and learn about a new place, but what about her family? She would miss them far too much. Also, there was the whole issue of school. She would have to change right in the middle of the year. How crazy would that be? She would be a stranger among people who already knew each other. Also, she would have to move in with people she would not know or would most likely not know. All this made Clem really want to stay at home and live her normal life.

Then again, if she didn't go, she would be letting Scarlett down and who knew how that would affect their friendship? Also, she wouldn't be able to tell her grandchildren, "You know, I went to Asia and bunked with a wonderful family while I learned loads about the history of the place." She didn't quite know why that was important to her, but for some reason, it was. She would also still be able to stay in touch with her family via email, phone, and letters, but then again, the exchange would last until June, which was six months from now. It would be half a year away from her family. Yet, she knew if she didn't like it, she could always just tell her family and come right home.

So many decisions, so little time.

She had looked over the papers, and it sounded like a pretty good deal. The main attraction was that if she didn't like it, she could go home. Of course, she also knew that there was a chance that she and her best friend might end up in different places. Clem was afraid of that. But then again, the more she thought about it, the more she began to like the idea of traveling to a far away place. After all, the furthest she had ever traveled in her fifteen years of life was Disney World in Florida, and that wasn't even really that far away. *Maybe*, Clem thought, *it's time for a change.*

Clem could hardly believe she'd slept any that night, but she knew she must have because the annoying buzz of her alarm clock woke her and all her troubles started again.

"Mom?" Clem asked, sliding into her chair for breakfast.

"Don't be so loud! The twins are still sleeping," she said in a pointed voice.

Uh-oh, Clem thought, *she's in a bad mood. That's not a good sign.*

"Sorry. Hey, Mom? Can you answer a question for me?"

Mrs. Greenly stopped cutting up apples for the triplets' lunches and looked at Clem in a very suspicious way. "It depends," she said and continued to chop.

Clem let out a nervous breath. "Well, what if the question was based on, uh, travel?" she asked.

Mrs. Greenly didn't look up. "What are you talking about, Clem? You hate travel."

"Ah-ha! You may say I hate travel, but what if I said that 'hate' can turn into 'hated'?" Clem asked.

Mrs. Greenly seemed to get fed up. "Clem, just ask me the question before I blow a gasket," she said, putting the knife in the dishwasher.

Clem sighed. "Fine. I ... I just wanted to know if I could join this ... thing." *What?* she asked herself, *What am I doing?*

"You mean a *travel* thing?" Mrs. Greenly asked.

"Well, yes. It's a foreign exchange program and it sounds really fun," Clem said.

Mrs. Greenly turned around and stared at her daughter. "*You?* Honey, last time I checked, travel wasn't even part of your vocabulary; it

The Lopsided Miracle

was ruled out. Now all of a sudden you want to be part of an exchange program?" She crossed her arms. "Baby, I know when something is wrong. Now spill."

Clem had no other choice. She told her mother all about Scarlett and her desperate desire to get away from home because her parents were getting a divorce.

Mrs. Greenly was surprised. "Marty and Mina? Goodness, you would think those two were as happy as larks!"

Clem told her mother how Scarlett wanted to go on this foreign exchange program so that she could just get away. Clem also told her mother that the only way Scarlett was going to go was if Clem was right there with her.

While hearing all of this, Mrs. Greenly had made all three triplets' lunches, put dishwashing detergent in the dishwasher, and poured herself a cup of coffee, but she had been listening.

"Well, gosh, Clem. That seems to be a bit of a poor bargain. I mean, you don't even like travel. Are you sure that there isn't any other way you can help her?" Mrs. Greenly asked.

"Mom, trust me. If I don't do this thing, Scarlett will have it hanging over my head for the rest of our friendship," Clem replied. "Besides, some of it isn't even Scarlett. Think about it, I'll be able to travel to a new place, meet new people ... "

"I don't know, Clem. How long is this for?"

"Uh ..." Clem was afraid her mother would definitely say no if she told her how long it was for. But then again, if her mother said no, then she wouldn't have to go, which had a certain appeal, too. Then, she wouldn't feel guilty about not going. "It's for six months."

"Six months!" Mrs. Greenly widened her eyes to the point where they looked like olives. "I'm sorry, Clem, no way."

"But, Mom ..."

"No." And that was that. Throughout breakfast, Clem was thinking that now she had a perfectly good excuse (besides her dislike

Emily E. Shipp

of traveling) not to go, but what if Scarlett didn't believe her? *Well, she's just going to have to,* Clem thought. She must have been crazy during those few moments yesterday and the night before when she thought she might want to go on the foreign exchange program. The only place for her was here, at home—with or without Scarlett beside her.

~

Ben came down to breakfast in a very befuddled mood. He had not yet brushed his hair or teeth, and he was still in his bathrobe. Mrs. Queenly had come upon Ben and Jodie so quickly, that both of them felt confused. Their parents, on the other hand, felt differently.

"Good morning, Benjamin!" his mother greeted him.

He plopped down in a chair and smiled weakly up at her. "Mornin'," he said dully. She sat down directly across from him with a bowl of oatmeal in her hands.

"So darling, have you made a decision yet?" she asked him.

He heaved a grunt. "No, and will you *please* stop asking me that every time I see you?"

"Well, I'm so sorry, but it's the only thing on our minds," she pointed out.

"Don't remind me," he grumbled.

"Well, I personally think it's a wonderful idea. I always wanted to do it as a child, but your grandmother and grandfather did not want a stranger in the house. You aren't being very open-minded," she said, taking a sip of tea.

"Thanks, Mom," he said and got up to take a bowl out of the cupboard. "I don't know; it's just that the idea is so forward—not to mention the fact that it's coming from Mrs. Queenly."

"Oh, listen, I don't really have a liking for her either, but you have to admit, it is a good idea."

"For her, yes, but all she wants is the money that would come in from the press if the news got wind of what we were doing—if we are

The Lopsided Miracle

doing it," he said, shaking cereal out of the box. "And she was so rude about it! I mean, she was practically screaming at us because her two stars were fading."

"I know, but you might have to look past that," she said, getting up. "What does your sister think about it?"

He shrugged.

"Oh, well, maybe you should talk to her. Listen, I'm going to go do a load of laundry while my oatmeal cools, so if you need me, I'll be collecting clothes." She left the room with her usual flourish. Ben sighed, wishing that he had never tried out for the role of the handsome character that happened to be the star of the TV show with the most uptight creator.

"What?" Jodie snapped through the door.

"Get up," Ben commanded.

"Why? It's too early," she complained.

"Jodie, it's 11:30," he said, checking his watch.

"Oh," she grunted. Ben heard sheets rustling and her slippers shuffling against the carpet. She opened the door and stared at him. She had her hair pulled up into a messy ponytail and her robe was slipped on in a lazy fashion. Her eyes were tired and she looked weak. She always looked tired in the morning, even if she had gone to bed at 10:00 and slept until 11:30 the next morning.

"This isn't a good time ..." she started to say, but Ben barged right in. She lifted her hand up and then dropped it in an aggravated manner. "Won't you come in?" she said sarcastically.

"We need to talk," he said, dropping down on the bed. "It's about the exchange program."

At this, Jodie rolled her eyes and fell into her rolling chair by the desk, which was not used for homework but for painting her nails, applying makeup, and so forth. "Do you know what I'm going to do?" she asked.

Emily E. Shipp

"What?" he asked.

She pushed over a couple of bottles of nail polish while reaching for the black polish. "I'm going to paint my nails black, and then I'm going to use my black eye liner for lip liner, too," she said, opening the bottle.

Ben groaned. "Jodie, I'm serious! The deadline is in two days and Mrs. Queenly is coming by tomorrow to check up on us. I don't know about you, but I don't really want to see her face any more often than necessary."

Jodie slammed the nail polish remover down on her desk. "Ben! I don't want to spend my day off school thinking about that stupid exchange program, okay? I hate it. It's driving me up the wall," she said, pulling out a cotton ball from a cup painted with a variety of different polishes.

"I don't mean to bug you, but won't it just nag at your brain until you make a decision?" he asked. Jodie pretended she hadn't heard him. "Jodie, think about it. We need to make a decision."

"I know!" she yelled, not taking her eyes off of her thumbnail, which was now completely black. She started to blow on it. "If you want to make a decision so quickly, then just take up the offer," she said, grabbing the wand to the black bottle again.

Ben was taken by surprise. "W-what?" he asked.

Jodie looked up as if she said this every day. "Ben, I am totally and completely serious. I mean, we just have to let this person stay with us; we can lend her or him the guest room and then *bam*. In a few months, everything is back to normal again."

Ben thought about this. She did have a point, but she seemed so relaxed about it. How did she do it?

It was a couple of moments after he was thinking this when he realized that he had said it out loud. Jodie laughed and stood up.

"Ben, when you're a girl with school, a job, and a boss who won't take any crap, then you've got to know how to pick your battles. Give

The Lopsided Miracle

Mom the paperwork. Today, all I want to think about is sun, fun, and the fact that I have no homework." Then she walked into her bathroom to find the hair dryer to blow her nails dry.

Ben looked after his sister and then smiled. She had a point. What was the big deal? She had practically said that maybe it would be fun to have an exchange student here. After all, what's the worst that could happen? He or she was just a person like Jodie or Ben (except for the acting bit). It would be something new. Ben just wished the timing of the idea was much better planned, but Jodie was right. There was no use in worrying about something that was supposed to be fun in the first place.

Mrs. Clavis walked through the door and smiled at Ben. "Does your sister have any dirty clothes?" she asked.

Ben shrugged. "Why would I know?" he asked, getting up and walking to the door. He stopped midway. "Oh, and by the way, the forms for the exchange program are on the desk in the den. They're due on Friday."

40

CHAPTER FOUR

"What do you *mean* you can't go?" Scarlett practically screamed in Clem's ear. "I can't go by myself! Have you begged on your knees yet?"

"Yes," Clem said, which was a huge lie. All she had done was ask, and when her mother had said no, that was the end of it. But Clem didn't want to go, so she saw no point in begging.

"*Clementine*! I swear I'm going to call you that for the rest of your life if you don't go!" Scarlett warned.

Clem leaned forward on the steps in front of her school. "I told you already, Scarlett, my mom said I can't go and I can't argue!" she exclaimed.

Scarlett moaned and plopped her head in her hands. "This is going to be disastrous!" she wailed. "If I go by myself then what will I do if I meet everyone at my new school and they all hate me?"

"That won't happen," Clem assured her.

"No, but what if it *does*?" Scarlett flailed her arms up and tilted her head toward the sky. "My reputation will be ruined before I even create one!"

"Scarlett, you are being melodramatic," Clem said.

"Yeah, right. You sound just like my mother," Scarlett said.

"Well, it's true—you are being stubborn. You're being so incredibly ..."

In the next few seconds, Scarlett's sad, depressed face slowly turned into a bright and inspired one. It was like magic how someone could change that quickly, from down to up faster than a rocket ship.

"What?" Clem asked.

Scarlett jumped up in the air. "That's *it*! Oh my gosh! I feel so *stupid*! Why oh *why* didn't I think of this *before*?" she asked herself.

Emily E. Shipp

Clem stood up, too. "Scarlett? What ..."

"My mom!" she pointed out, interrupting Clem. "If my mom talks to your mom about the whole situation, then she will have to let you go! Your mom is a soft person ... she'll let you go if my mom tells her what kind of shape I'm in. She has to!"

Clem creased her eyebrows at Scarlett's point of view. "Scarlett, I don't know..." Actually, she did know. She knew very well that her mother was a soft person and a polite person, too. If she spoke one word to Mrs. McIntyre then she would fall into Scarlett's trap, and Clem would be on the next flight to South America.

"Well, it's worth a shot!" Scarlett said. She eyed Clem suspiciously. "You do want to go, don't you?"

"Well ..."

"Exactly. I have a couple of quarters to call my mom about it, so I'll have to miss homeroom. Just tell Mr. Brown I'll be a little late, okay?" And before Clem could even stutter, Scarlett rocketed through the double doors of Omega Parsley High School with such speed anyone could have sworn she was on roller blades.

Clem massaged her temples and walked into school thinking about how much trouble this was causing in her life. Why did Scarlett insist that Clem come with her? Obviously, all it was causing was chaos and confusion.

After a long talk with Mr. Brown about Scarlett's tardiness and a long, rough class in which every two seconds someone asked Clem where Scarlett was, she was let out to go to her next class. She breathed a sigh of relief as she walked out, but then she stood nose-to-nose with Scarlett McIntyre.

"Hi!" she said cheerfully.

Clem growled. "Scarlett! Why weren't you in at *least* the last part of class?" she asked impatiently.

Scarlett let out a long breath. "Well ... because I called my mom and talked to her for about twenty minutes about the reason why your

The Lopsided Miracle

mom won't let you do the foreign exchange program, and then my mom called your mom, and thirty minutes later she called me back saying that with a little begging and pleading—actually she just said that she was polite about it, but I'm sure she begged and pleaded—your mom said ..." There was a huge silence. Clem was sure her heart was so loud that Scarlett could hear it. But Scarlett just smiled broadly and squealed while giving Clem a hyper hug.

"Yes!" she squealed with excitement. "She said you could come with me! She did! She *did*! I'm so *happy!* Aren't you?" she shrieked happily.

Clem just stood in silence with only one thought on her mind: *How could my mom be so stupid?*

"You don't look very happy," Scarlett observed.

Quickly, Clem pasted a fake smile on her face. "I couldn't be happier," she fibbed.

Scarlett beamed. "Oh, Clem. You have no idea how happy I am that I am finally getting away. I can feel my troubles getting lighter by the minute!" she exclaimed. Clem kept her fake grin perched on her face, but it took great skill to not blow up at that moment. "Well, I'd better be off to science. You know how she gets when I'm late. Besides, today we're making energy bars ... like I need them. Ha!" Scarlett said cheerfully as if she couldn't have cared less if she was late or not, as if energy bars were the most exciting things in the world. Clem watched, drained, as Scarlett skipped all the way down to the next hall.

All of a sudden, Clem felt dizzy, as if she needed very much to lie down. Luckily, her next class was right next door. She walked in and went straight to Mrs. Hartley's desk.

"Mrs. Hartley?" Clem asked.

The actress-like teacher looked up and smiled. "Well, hello, Clem! How is everything?"

"Well ..." Clem didn't really know what to say. "I ... just kind of feel sick. Can I please go to the nurse?" she asked.

Emily E. Shipp

Mrs. Hartley's smile left her face. "Oh, well, I suppose so. Here ..." she said, getting a blue hall pass from her desk drawer. "Here's a pass to go." She ripped off a pass and handed it to Clem. "Okay. Go on, but feel better—you wouldn't want to be sick for the math quiz Monday."

"Yeah, I wouldn't want to miss that," Clem said as sarcastically as she could manage. Mrs. Hartley was laughing when Clem left the room.

Clem knew what was wrong, but she didn't know why it was affecting her so much. Maybe it was because she would be away from her family for so long. Maybe it was because everything was happening way too fast, or maybe it was because she just completely hated the thought of travel. She just didn't know.

The walk to the nurse's office seemed to be the longest ever, but finally she arrived with a headache so big she thought she might explode.

When she staggered in, she saw the nurse (an old gray-haired lady with moles the size of Alaska on her big, hairy neck) talking on the phone to a sick patient's mother about picking her daughter up from school.

"Yes ... yes, Caroline is here ... No, it's not another case of pneumonia ..." she scratched out dully. Clem made her way quietly to the other side of the room where she saw the sick Caroline laying on a bed with plastic covering on it. Clem recognized her from her physical education class.

"Hey," Clem said, smiling at her.

"H-" Before any real talking progress was made, she hurled into a bucket already occupied with watery, food-filled liquid. Clem chose not to look at it before she threw up, too. Once Caroline had finished her "business," she gargled some nearby water, spat it out into the bucket, and wiped her mouth with a napkin. "Sorry you had to see that," she said, her unnaturally red hair swinging forward as she coughed.

The Lopsided Miracle

"It's okay. I didn't look at most of it," Clem said. Caroline laughed weakly.

Miss Right, the nurse, came back then and looked from Caroline to Clem. "When did you get here?" she asked Clem.

"Uh ... Mrs. Hartley sent me. I feel a little queasy," she said truthfully.

Miss Right rolled her eyes. "Oh, please don't tell me that. I've had all the sickness I can take for today," she said, gesturing toward the sick-looking Caroline.

"Well, it's more of a headache, actually," Clem said as her head began to pound again.

Miss Right sighed and looked over at Caroline. "Your mother said that she would be here in about twenty minutes." She looked the redhead up and down. "You don't look much like going to get your stuff, so if you want to, you can tell me one of your friend's names, and I'll go tell them to get your stuff."

Caroline coughed and then said, "Can you ask Rudy Montello to get my things, please?" Her eyes brightened when she said his name.

"Rudy, huh?" Miss Right looked at Caroline discouragingly. "Is this a boy we're talking about?"

"Yes, it's my boyfriend," she said. Miss Right shook her head and clucked her tongue as she skirted around the appliances in the office to head out to the front office.

Caroline looked at Clem. "Do you really feel queasy?" she asked.

Clem sighed. "Yes, but then again, my head is hurting, too," she told her.

Caroline smiled. "Why?" she asked.

"I don't know ... maybe it was something I ate. You should know how food can affect you," Clem said, knowing perfectly well that this was more than a hypothesis. "What's wrong with you?"

Emily E. Shipp

"I must've eaten something bad," Caroline said, bored. "I have a feeling it was that Hot Pocket I ate for br—" Clem turned away again as a fountain of spew appeared from Caroline's mouth. Clem gulped. "I think I need some fresh air," she said.

About twenty minutes later, Mrs. Greenly drove up in the minivan wearing a pair of jeans and a baseball cap and looking like the mother of the year. She walked into Omega Parsley with a concerned look on her face, and two babies on her hips.

"Clem?" She looked around the main office until she recognized her daughter, who was looking flushed and tired. "Clem!" She rushed over. Clem stood up and swung her backpack over her shoulder. "Are you alright, baby?" Mrs. Greenly asked.

"I don't feel well," Clem said for the thousandth time. "I have a headache."

Mrs. Greenly nodded and took Clem's backpack from her shoulder. "I'm sorry, dear. What happened?" she asked.

You betrayed me, Clem wanted to say, but that would make no sense because Mrs. Greenly thought that Clem wanted to go on the exchange program.

"I don't know. I guess it's just a homework overload or something," she improvised. "You know how the teachers always want everything turned in before the Christmas holidays."

"I do," Mrs. Greenly said, patting her daughter's cheek, "and I think a day off of school will not kill you or your teachers. How does a nice warm cup of tea sound?"

Clem smiled a bit. "It sounds soothing," she said, imagining herself lying in bed where other countries and airplanes did not exist.

They walked out to the van. Clem headed for the passenger seat while her mother put away her backpack in the back of the vehicle. When the back came open, Clem saw the collection of bumper stickers placed proudly beside the license plate. There was one for every child of the Greenly family. The "I'm A Soccer Mom!" sticker had been the very

The Lopsided Miracle

first, in honor of Stephen, who had played soccer ever since he was five. Then Clem came along and took up swimming, so Mrs. Greenly had stuck a swimming sticker on. But then Clem decided that swimming took up too much free time, so she quit, and once she was accepted into Omega Parsley High School, the swimming sticker had been covered up with the "My Child Is An Omega Parsley Kid!" sticker. Then the triplets came. Beverly, obviously, was not much of a sporting person, yet she loved to ride horseback, so that's where the "I'm Proud To Be A Horseback Rider!" sticker came from. For Bailey, who loved basketball, there was the "Shoot For The Gold! My Kid Is A Basketball Star!" sticker, and for brainy Brooke, of course, there was the "My Child Is The Winner Of The Roberson White Elementary Valedictorian Award!"

Clem was so caught up in thinking about the stickers that she hardly noticed her mother put the twins in the car seats. Tommy and Travis were so exhausted, they fell asleep right away.

"Are you sure it's a headache?" Mrs. Greenly whispered, trying not to wake the twins. "You look a little flushed."

Clem nodded. She closed her eyes and wondered if she should ask her mother now about the exchange program, but with one look at her mother—who was already more concerned about Clem's well-being than anything else—her conscience told her not to bring it up until later.

When they finally reached the house, a chilly wind had begun to blow. All of a sudden, Clem very much wanted to see the ocean. That was one of the many great things about living in South Carolina: The ocean was right there.

Mrs. Greenly parked and opened the car door, retrieving Travis, who now had a small stream of drool flowing down the side of his mouth.

"Clem, honey, could you do me a big favor?" she asked. Without waiting for an answer, she continued, "Could you please get your backpack out and bring it in for me? I would ask you to grab one of the

Emily E. Shipp

twins, but I don't want them catching anything you have if it's contagious." She unbuckled Tommy's seatbelt. He was still dead asleep, but Travis was just beginning to open his eyes in his mother's arms.

"Sure, Mom," Clem said, opening the trunk and taking one last glance at the bumper stickers before she shut the back again and moved swiftly inside the house.

When she opened the door, she felt a cool blast of air from the air conditioner. She paused a moment, smelling the leather from the furniture in the nearby living room and the Lysol that always filled the house because the twins were always spreading germs, and took in the look of the modern silver, black, and white everything from the foyer to the kitchen. She took it all in, saving the picture in her mind and storing it in her head so that she could look at it again when she was gone and needed a reminder that her family was still there, in the same place. She knew that she would come back one day to greet it all again.

"I'm so sorry ... really, I am," Chelsea said, bringing up more tea for Clem. "I hope you feel better."

"I'll be fine. It's just a little bug," Clem replied. Chelsea was Stephen's new girlfriend. She was blonde and pretty and absolutely adored his brothers and sisters.

"It's just now that you're sick, I feel really bad taking Stephen out to dinner. Shouldn't he be here, helping you get better?" she asked.

"No, no, really. I'll be fine, and besides that, the absolute most Stephen *ever* does for me when I'm sick is tell me to stay out of his face so that he doesn't catch it, too."

Chelsea laughed aloud. "Well, okay. If you say so," she said. She walked out of the room, still smiling at Clem's comment.

Clem sighed and lay back against her pillows, replaying the scene with her mother in her head. A couple hours after Clem was first bedridden with her headache, her mother came in with lunch. She sat

The Lopsided Miracle

there for a moment on a white, fuzzy butterfly chair beside Clem's bed before making the announcement.

"Well, I don't know if Scarlett already told you or not, but ..." She seemed a little uncomfortable. "Your father and I have decided to let you go ahead and try out this foreign exchange program you wanted to go on," she said.

Clem didn't know what to do. After all, she had been faking her eagerness. Finally, after moments of silence, Clem put down her grilled cheese sandwich and washed it down with some milk before speaking.

"Mom ... I sort of lied to you," Clem said, feeling uncomfortable.

Mrs. Greenly looked surprised. "Really? How so?" she asked.

Clem took a deep breath. "Well, I didn't really want to go on the exchange program. It's just that Scarlett wanted me to go so badly and ..." All of a sudden, Mrs. Greenly put her hand up, signaling for Clem to stop talking.

"I know," she said, looking deep into Clem's eyes. "I know how those friendships are. After all, I had a best friend once, and the kind of friend who will do something she hates for a friend's sake is the best kind of friend in my book."

Clem furrowed her eyebrows. "So, you're saying I should still go?" she asked. "You don't want me here?"

"Clem!" Mrs. Greenly was shocked. "What are you talking about? Of course I want you here! I wouldn't be able to live without you; you *know* that," she said, taking Clem's chin in her hand. "But I also know that you have a friend in need, and I don't think you would be very much of a friend if you didn't help her out."

Clem felt her mother take her hand away. "I know, Mom. But what if I really, really, really don't want to go?" she asked.

Mrs. Greenly stood up. "Then I guess you don't have to go," she said, looking thoughtful. "But think about poor Scarlett ... what if you were in her shoes?" Mrs. Greenly stared at Clem for a long time until finally she turned around and started walking out.

Emily E. Shipp

    Just as she was reaching the doorway, Clem spoke quickly after her. "Wait!"

    Mrs. Greenly turned around to meet her gaze. "Yes?" she asked.

    "Well ... as long as I can come back if I don't like it ... promise?" Clem asked.

    Mrs. Greenly smiled broadly and started laughing. "Oh, Clem! You know that is a promise," she said. Clem smiled and her mother walked back and embraced her with a hug. "Clem... you know that you are doing the right thing." Mrs. Greenly spoke as if she were Confucius on estrogen.

    Clem closed her eyes. *Let's hope so*, she thought.

~

    "One, two, one, two, *three, four*!" Ryan Matthews called out, tapping his drumsticks together. Ryan, Ben, and Mark Olshire all burst into song: Ryan on the drums, Mark on the keyboard, and Ben on the guitar as the lead singer.

    "*I like those clothes, but they don't fit, I like that hemp, don't have the kit ...*" Ben sang. "*I want those shoes, don't know the price, want my life? Well, it ain't nice ...*" They sang and sang in Ryan's large garage until sweat beads rolled down their faces. This is the way it always was—it was just like old times.

    The band (Three's No Crowd) had been started about a month after *The Truth Told by Me* had begun. The guys had gotten to know each other better, and once they all figured out that they loved music, they decided to form a small band, and they had succeeded—only playing for pleasure, though. They didn't really want pressure getting in the way of their band—or their friendship.

    "*... Sure there are some things I really want, but nothing is better than ...*" The song came to an end without a closing word. All at once, the band broke out into applause.

The Lopsided Miracle

"Thank you ... Thank you ..." Ben pretended to bow to a loving audience. "Have a good night and drive safely!" he said.

"Oh, come on, Ben. You know it's not *you* they want," Mark said, flipping a switch on the keyboard and moving his brown hair out of his eyes.

"Oh, yeah, and so who else is there to love?" Ben asked.

"Me, dork," Ryan said, doing a stunning drum routine and ending with a clash of cymbals.

"Yeah, yeah, yeah," Ben said, taking off his guitar. He walked over to the bench where their provisions were held. "Who wants Skittles?"

"Me ... and no lemons!" Ryan yelled. Ben laughed.

"No, just chocolate for me," Mark said, leaving his keyboard and picking up a King Size pack of M&Ms.

"How can you even process the idea of eating chocolate when you have Skittles? The world's number one candy!" Ryan said, joining the two at the bench.

"I can *process* it because I'm always thinking about it anyway," Mark replied. Ryan laughed.

They all sat down in various "guy" positions, flicking candies into their mouths when all of a sudden, Mark asked, "So ... who do you think you guys are going to get as the exchange student?"

Ben sighed. "I don't know. I don't want to think about it. I'm only doing it because I'm getting paid extra," he said.

Ryan huffed. "I still can't believe you're getting paid *double* to have some person stay in your house. I mean, all you have to do is stay out of their way and you're home free!" Ryan burped. No one seemed to care.

"Yeah, but it will most likely be a "she" who won't stop hanging over me. Not that I'm trying to gloat or anything, but really. Do I want some haywire fan hanging on my every breath?" he asked rhetorically. He had no idea he was being egotistical.

Emily E. Shipp

"Well, there is just one thing you can hope for," Ryan said, smiling.

Ben raised his eyebrow. "Oh, yeah? And what would that be?"

Ryan took a drink of Coke. "Hope she's French, dude," he said, laughing. Mark spit out the Coke he was drinking and started snorting with laughter.

Ben rolled his eyes. "You guys are sick," he said. They just continued with their hysterical laughter as Ben popped another Skittle into his mouth.

Just like old times, he thought, *the only place I'll be able to be at home anymore.*

Ben wasn't the only one thinking about it. Jodie was at home, working on homework while her mother was in the other room, making decisions about the exchange student.

"Yes, I know. I think we'll have the guest room for her or him. Mmmhmmmm ...," she said, writing things down on a notepad. Jodie grunted and put her head in her hands.

It was all everyone talked about. It was all everyone thought about. Yet, Jodie had to admit it was very exciting.

Maybe it will be someone who, for once, doesn't look up to Ben, Jodie thought, rolling her eyes. That was the way it always was: Ben first and Jodie second. When opening presents on Christmas morning, Ben always went first. When Jodie wanted a new bike, Ben got one first because he was older. When Jodie and Ben both tried out for *The Truth Told by Me*, Ben snagged the lead and Jodie was the co-star. And those were only a few examples.

This time it was going to be different. Jodie was going to be part of this, too. She was going to be in the news *along with* Ben. It wasn't all about him this time. She was going to be there.

The Lopsided Miracle

"Yes ... Okay, thank you, Mrs. Queenly. I'll see you when I pick up the forms," Jodie's mother said then hung up the phone. She walked into the living room with her arms down to her sides.

"Oh! This is going to be exciting, don't you think, darling?" Mrs. Clavis asked.

Jodie nodded. "Yeah, it'll definitely be different," she said.

Mrs. Clavis smiled to herself, not really paying much attention to Jodie. "I'm just so overwhelmed! That's the only problem! I've never done this before, and I just don't know where to begin!" she exclaimed, falling on the couch next to where Jodie was working. "And along with all of this, Barbara just called and told me that I'm the only one who's up for holding my book club's annual dinner! I didn't even have time to tell her that I can't do it. So now I have even more on my plate than I bargained for! Ah," she breathed. For a couple of seconds, she just sat on the couch in deep thought while Jodie worked on her math problems. Then Mrs. Clavis spoke suddenly.

"I need to make a checklist," she said, hopping up and going down the hall and up the steps to retrieve a piece of paper from her bedroom. Jodie just smiled after her mother and continued to work.

About fifteen minutes later, though, Ben came in from band practice at Ryan's. His face was flushed from the chilly fall wind, and his hair was severely windblown. Jodie waited until he came down the hall and into the living room before she spoke to him.

"Hi," she said, not taking her eyes off of her homework.

"Hullo," he said, flopping on the couch. "We were great today."

"That's good," Jodie said.

"Oh, and Ryan asked if he could go out with you," Ben said, trying to distract Jodie.

Jodie sighed. "No. No, no, no. That is my answer every time you come home from practice. The answer is and will always be no," she said.

Emily E. Shipp

Ben chuckled. "I know, he just always wants to give it a shot," he said.

Jodie laughed, too. "He's cool," she said. "very funny."

"Oh?" Ben looked surprised. "Well I'll just have to tell him that next time we practice."

"Ah!" she said, smiling playfully as she kicked him in the shin.

"Ow!" Hey, no fair. I have a bruise there," he said, pointing to it.

Jodie laughed. "Yep, and I think I gave you that one, too." She grinned. They didn't talk for a while. Jodie did not want to because she needed to finish her homework. Ben, rested up from his long bike ride back, decided to do his, too.

"I'm leaving," he said, getting up.

"I won't miss you," Jodie said. That was the way their relationship as brother and sister worked. They were friends one minute and rivals the next.

"Ha, ha," Ben said, without an ounce of enthusiasm. He trotted up the stairs, his feet making little *pat, pat* noises on the carpeted steps. He looked over the banister at Jodie, working in the living room and not knowing he was there.

On the way to his room, he saw the guest bedroom at the end of the hall. The door was cracked open. He hadn't seen it since they fixed it up a bit for the exchange student. Full of curiosity, he walked over to the bedroom and pushed open the door.

It was almost empty. There was the plain, white four-poster bed with a naked mattress sitting atop of it. Then there was a white bureau with nothing in the drawers and nothing atop of it either. The carpet was vacuumed, and there weren't even hangers in the closet. That was it: an empty bed and an empty bureau.

Ben walked out of the room feeling happy. He was about to dive into the depths of a new risk—something he did often. And now, he couldn't wait for the exchange student to get there.

CHAPTER FIVE

Clem jerked up her head from her desk. She had almost fallen asleep. When she heard her name over the P.A. system, she shook her head back to life and listened for the rest of the announcement.

"Teachers, pardon the interruption, but would Alex Bridget, Clem Greenly, Sally Jewen, Loren Lust, and Scarlett McIntyre please report to the front office immediately? Thank you." Then the principal's voice shut off as the announcement came to a close. Everyone in the class looked at Clem, and she looked up at Mrs. Hartley.

"Go ahead, Clem," she said. Clem nodded and picked herself up. Making her way out of the room, she saw Scarlett coming down the hall, too. She was beaming.

"Isn't this exciting?" she asked as soon as she caught up to Clem. "We get to find out where we're going!" She jumped up and down like a Mexican jumping bean.

"Oh." Clem caught on. Actually, she had no idea that they were receiving their destinations that day. All of a sudden, she was excited, too. She smiled. "I hope we get to go someplace exotic like Namibia," she said, dreaming about it.

"Oh, I know—me too," Scarlett said, still hyper as they made their way down the hall. "I mean, what if we get to go someplace like Australia? Wouldn't that be great!" she said, obviously daydreaming like Clem.

"Yeah," Clem replied. They continued to walk down the squeaky-clean halls of Omega Parsley until they reached the front office. The woman working there looked at them. She seemed mad and crabby.

"Are you two of the exchange students?" she asked. She was very old and had her hair in loose, frizzy curls all around her head. Clem looked at the woman's nametag—Ms. Ringleight. The two girls

Emily E. Shipp

nodded at the woman. She looked at them sternly and then pulled out five manila envelopes from a desk drawer.

"Names?" she asked gruffly.

"Scarlett McIntyre," Scarlett rushed to reply. Ms. Ringleight thumbed through the envelopes until she reached the one she was looking for. She handed it to Scarlett.

Then Ms. Ringleight looked at Clem. "Name?" she asked.

Clem swallowed. "Clem Greenly," she said. This time the woman didn't take long at all. It was the envelope on the very top. Clem looked at it. It was blank with only her name written in permanent marker on the front.

"Now, you two aren't to look at these until you are at home with a parent," Ms. Ringleight said. "And you'd better do as I say."

The two girls nodded again and then set off down the hall. They looked at each other, knowing that at next break they would meet in the girls' bathroom and open the envelopes there.

Class seemed to take forever to end, but, alas, it did, and Clem and Scarlett were both jittery as they met in the bathroom. Clem checked under the doors of the stalls to make sure no one was there while Scarlett applied clear, wet lip gloss that left her finger sticky. She grabbed a paper towel and wiped it off.

"Is anyone here?" Scarlett asked Clem as she checked the last stall.

"No, not a soul," Clem said, swallowing hard. "This is probably going to sound stupid, but I'm a little nervous." She clutched her plain, denim skirt.

"It doesn't sound stupid at all," Scarlett reassured her. "I'm nervous, too." They waited a long time until finally Scarlett cleared her throat. "Well, don't just stand there like an idiot. Open it," she said.

Clem jumped at the mere thought of going first. "Me? No ... you go. You're the one who wanted to do this whole thing in the first place," she said. There, now Scarlett couldn't say no. She obviously felt the

The Lopsided Miracle

same way, so she smiled weakly and slowly started to tear open the top. *Slowly* being the key word. Clem thought she was going to bust if Scarlett didn't hurry up.

"Come *on*, Scarlett. I haven't got all day! Class starts in two minutes!" she said, hearing the bustle of the students still outside in the halls.

"Okay, okay!" She made the last rip. "It's open!" she proclaimed, taking the forms out of the envelope. She skimmed through a couple sentences on the first page and then a smile split across her face.

"Listen!" she said. "*Dear Miss McIntyre, we are pleased to inform you that you have been accepted by the Montreal family in London, England!*" she read happily. She giggled and then ran over and hugged Clem tightly. "Yes!"

"Wait!" Clem said, still a little scared by the butterflies in her stomach. "I still have to open mine."

"Oh, right." Scarlett tried to calm down, but it took much effort. "Go ahead!" she urged.

Clem looked quickly from her best friend to the envelope. Then she understood why Scarlett had taken so long to open the package. About twenty seconds later, the top was open, and Clem was afraid to take out its contents.

"Come on, Clem, you know you're going to be somewhere near me! I just want to know what the family sounds like," Scarlett said happily. "Now let's get a move on!" She sounded just like a teacher.

Clem smiled a bit, remembering that she *was* going to be close to Scarlett, and then took out the plain, white sheet of paper with plain, black, Times New Roman print on it. "*Dear Miss Greenly,*" she read aloud. "*We are pleased to inform you that you have been accepted by the Clavis family in ...*" Her eyes turned as round as golf balls. "*Toronto, Canada?*"

Emily E. Shipp

"Canada?" Scarlett repeated. "*Canada*! That must be at least a zillion miles away from London!"

It was the first time they had been able to talk since Clem had read the letter out loud in the women's bathroom. Right after she had read the words on that evil sheet of paper, a teacher had come in and asked them both to get to class. Now it was lunch and these were the first words on the matter. Scarlett had plenty to say, but the whole thing left Clem speechless.

"I mean, come on!" Scarlett said. "You would *think* they would put us at least on the same *continent*! But no! Not to mention that this is not just some vacation! This is for *six months*! Six months away from my best friend!" She rolled her head up to the sky. "If I have ever believed in fate, all of it has gone down the drain."

Clem opened and closed her mouth several times, but still could not find words. Finally she just picked up her milk carton and took a sip. At least it was something to keep her mouth busy.

"I won't be able to see you!" Scarlett trailed on, "and I won't have anyone to fall back on if I make a fool of myself in my new school! I won't have anyone, *anyone* to tell secrets to if I have a new crush on somebody! And ..." She reached over and grabbed Clem's arm, gasping suddenly as if she had just thought of something horrible. "What if I can't speak the language? What if no one speaks English? What if I do something wrong like wear the wrong kind of nail polish and they start laughing at me in *French*?!" She let go of Clem's arm and clutched her shirt where her heart was located. "I'm doomed!"

"No, you're not." Finally, Clem had something to say. "I'm sure most people speak English there, I mean it's *England*... and you don't have to worry about me." Clem's eyes clouded over. "I'm sure you'll make a new best friend in no time." She spoke quietly.

Scarlett looked at Clem with an expression of absolute mortification plastered on her face. "Clem," she breathed. "Clem ... you don't really believe that, do you?" Clem didn't answer. "I could never

The Lopsided Miracle

replace you! Even if I do make new friends, I could never, ever replace someone as important as you!"

Clem looked at Scarlett. Radiant red hair, glimmering eyes, and a concerned brow were the best features of her very best friend. All of a sudden, Clem had to try very hard to keep tears out of her eyes, and even trying her very hardest wasn't enough.

"Oh, Scarlett! I'm going to miss you so much!" she said, tears spilling out of the corners of her eyes, making everything blurry, "And... I just want to say I'm really, really sorry... but I appreciate everything..."

Scarlett, seeing her best friend breaking down, started to cry, too. She reached over and gave Clem a hug, even tighter than when she was happy, because now it was a hug she would have to remember. "I'll *never* forget you, Clem Greenly," she said, wiping a salty drip from her eye. "Not even in six months."

"Canada? Well, isn't that exciting!" Mrs. Greenly said, reading the forms. "I think it's going to be a great experience for you, even if Scarlett isn't there."

"That's not what I wanted to hear," Clem mumbled. She had hoped her mother would say something like *Well, since Scarlett isn't even going to be in the same general vicinity then maybe you shouldn't go after all,* or *Well, Canada is so boring, why don't you just stay here, and we'll do something else*? No. Instead, she had said, "Well, since we've already paid for it, it will still be a wonderful experience!"

What was up with her mother and "wonderful experiences"?

Well, whatever it was, it was bugging Clem a lot. Now she really didn't want to go because she wouldn't even be near Scarlett.

Clem's mother flapped down the papers and looked Clem's way—obviously miffed.

"Well, then, what did you want me to say?" she asked, raising an eyebrow.

Emily E. Shipp

Clem sighed. "I don't know," she said, picking at a nail. "Something to keep me from going."

Mrs. Greenly laughed. "That'll be the day," she said.

Clem looked up, shocked. "Mom! I thought you said it was my choice!" she said.

Mrs. Greenly sucked in air. "Well, it is, sweetie," she said, letting all the air out. "But I just think I would never forgive myself if I didn't encourage you to go. After all, you never know—you might actually like it."

Clem snorted. "That'll be the day," she said.

Mrs. Greenly smiled in spite of her daughter's stubbornness. "Here," she said, handing some of the forms to Clem. "Here's some information about the family. I haven't gotten a chance to read about them yet, but I'm sure you'll want to take a peek at them first."

Clem didn't say anything. She knew that if she started to say something sarcastic about this remark, she would never stop. Mrs. Greenly got up and left the room to go check on Tommy and Travis, who were both screaming about something that was obviously also affecting Beverly because Clem could hear her screaming, too. Clem paid no attention to the familiar racket and took one glance at the picture they sent. It wasn't even really a glance; it was more like a rushed roll of the eye. She hadn't seen the family... yet.

It was about two o'clock in the morning and Clem was wiped out. She was having a strange dream about acorns and bumper stickers, two things she did not long to leave behind, when all of a sudden Bailey woke her up by shaking her. Clem looked up. Bailey was flushed. Her hair was sticking to her forehead with sweat, and she looked utterly shocked.

"Clem ... *Clem* ... Wake *up!*" she said in a loud whisper.

"What, what ... what is it, Bailey? Can't it wait until morning ...?"

The Lopsided Miracle

"*No*! Clem, this is *serious!* I stole your paperwork from your desk a couple of minutes ago; you know—the paperwork about the family in Toronto? Didn't you look at the picture?" she asked urgently.

Clem was so tired she could hardly think, much less comprehend what her sister was trying to say to her. "What?" she asked again.

"Here!" Bailey said, shoving the picture into Clem's hands. Clem squinted as she turned on the lamp on the bedside table. She sat up in bed and looked at it.

There was a nice-looking, normal family: a beautiful woman with perfect blonde hair and a man with perfect, lovely looking teeth. Then, Clem stared at the two children in the picture.

And Jodie and Ben Clavis, national television stars, stared right back at her.

~

Ben lay on the couch. A severe case of gloom hovered over him while a large, overstuffed manila envelope lay beside him.

"Ben! Dinner!" his mother called. He didn't think he could move, much less get up for a pointless thing like dinner.

"I'm not hungry," he said frankly. He heard a pot crash into the sink.

"Well, I'm sure your sister is, so go up and get her," she said. Ben still didn't move. He didn't want to. He simply wanted to reverse time to the point where Mrs. Queenly had come to visit. Then he could have said no to the exchange student program idea, and he wouldn't be in this big mess.

"Ben ..." He heard his mother's warning voice and rolled his eyes.

"Fine," he grunted, getting up and slouching into the foyer where the stairs were located. He trudged up them and carelessly knocked on Jodie's door.

"What?" she asked.

Emily E. Shipp

"Dinner," he grumbled.

"Oh," she said. The conversation was so familiar ... all that was going to be destroyed. That was the only thought running through his head these days. How everything that seemed familiar at home was going to be different because someone else was going to intrude ... and not just someone as in anyone. Someone as in the biggest fan Ben had ever had—Clementine Greenly.

Jodie opened the door, and Ben realized he was still standing there. She gave him a funny look and then brushed past him and swiftly moved down the stairs. Ben closed his eyes and moved his head back, cracking his neck. He never thought he would consider a day at an aromatherapy spa. But maybe some fragrances would relieve his stress.

Of course, he thought, making his way to his room because he felt if he ate anything it would just come right back up, *I thought this was going to be exciting. But of course, I was wrong*.

He opened his door and then shut it, locked it, and shoved a chair under the knob because Jodie knew the trick to unlock it. He then turned around and let loose all his muscles, falling on the bed and hoping he would suffocate in the pillow. His life was over anyway.

He could not process the idea that Clem was coming. She would follow his every move; she would completely ruin his social life. He knew about fans. In fact, there was one fan who went to his middle school, and that was a nightmare. She started wearing a "BEN CLAVIS FOR PRESIDENT" shirt, with his face instead of Uncle Sam's in the old "I want YOU" pose. When she started making Ben Clavis buttons, he knew he had to get away fast.

Let's just hope she's not as creative with clothes as that girl, he thought miserably. He rolled over and breathed in the smell of the one-dollar scented tree sachets that were meant for his car, but instead were used to stink up his room. That smell was mixed with millions of empty

The Lopsided Miracle

peppermint wrappers, deodorant, and various materials scattered around the room, such as rubber bands and lead from pencils.

He needed a getaway. He grabbed his keys from the messy desk covered with glue, crumpled papers, pencil shavings—everything he never bothered to clean up. But then he decided he wasn't going to use his car today. He was going to use his bike instead. He didn't want to concentrate on driving; he just wanted to let go and speed down the hill as fast as he could. He threw his keys on the floor and went out the window.

So much for not being able to wait until she gets here, he thought, climbing down the vine-covered gate on the side of the house. *If it means I'm going to have a girl who has been writing me once a week staying in my house and making me absolutely miserable like in my middle school days, then I think I'd rather pass.*

CHAPTER SIX

"What do you think?" Scarlett asked, tipping the beret so it cast a shadow over her eyes, and then made a sexy, pouting face.

"Well, it looks very ... French," Clem answered, shrugging.

Scarlett flipped it off with two fingers and threw it in her cart. "Good. I'm going to London, and London's in England, and Paris is nearby, too ... so it's basically the same thing," she said, waving the situation off and smiling at a red-and-white striped tie-up tee. "Oh! I *love* this! Doesn't it just scream foreign country?" she asked, holding it up to her chest.

Actually, it looked very American to Clem, but she didn't say anything bad about it. She just smiled and waved her hands in front of her. "Yes! I love it! Everyone will love you in that shirt." She gestured to it, grinning.

Scarlett grinned back. "Okay." She tossed it into the cart, too. She looked at Clem's empty cart. "What?! Clem, come on, this is supposed to be a shopping trip for our new clothes. After all, we're both going to colder climates," she pointed out. "None of my clothes will fit English weather. They're all too ... South Carolina- *ish*."

"I know, me too, and I need a new wardrobe for ... you know who," Clem said. Then they both squealed.

Scarlett laughed. "I still can't believe how lucky you are! I mean it's not that I like the guy ... but seriously! Living with a celebrity? Oh! I would so die to be you!"

Clem giggled. "I know. I can't believe it either! I'm going to be staying in the same house as Ben Clavis." She could hardly believe she was saying those words. She would never have thought she would be saying those words! And yet, here she was, saying them loud and proud.

Emily E. Shipp

"Well, if you're going to be staying with him and his folks for six months, then you need to pick out some new clothes, so come on! We have all day, yet so little time," she said, picking up a crocheted scarf. It was all earth colors and very pretty.

"Now this," Scarlett noted, "would go so well with that brown turtleneck we saw back there. It's made of almost the same material! Those two with these jeans ..." and on and on she went, which is why Clem spent $1,200 (and 50 cents) on clothes that day—all on her mother's credit card. Clem was sure her mother wasn't going to be happy when she saw the bill. *Oh well*, Clem thought, *at least I got enough outfits to last me three months, with a new outfit for each week!*

When the two reached Scarlett's house, Clem helped her carry everything into Scarlett's room (and Clem was sure Scarlett had spent even more than she had) and then unloaded everything from the bags. Clem was positive that an average person would have died to have the amount of clothes that Scarlett had bought. Clem wasn't worried about the cost, though, because it was Scarlett's own credit card and she had a three thousand dollar credit limit. She had probably spent more than half of it.

"I'm so glad I bought that beret," she said, picking up a blue midriff shirt (50% off!). "It goes perfectly with this shirt!"

"We had so much fun today," Clem said, letting her hair down from her ponytail and wrapping the elastic band around her wrist. "It was a great last shopping trip."

All of a sudden, the smile faded from Scarlett's quaint face. She looked down at her new black, strappy sandals with the clear band that still bound them together. Her red hair fell in front of her face as she swallowed hard.

"Yeah," she whispered. "It was a great ... last ... shopping trip."

Just looking at her best friend made Clem want to dissolve into tears, like she did in the cafeteria. She blinked them back and tried to smile—but it only came weakly. "Hey, it's not forever, don't worry," Clem

The Lopsided Miracle

assured her. "We'll see each other again, and we'll be able to have even more shopping trips when we get back."

Scarlett laughed through her muffled tears. "Yeah," she said, sniffling and wiping the tears away, "and we'll write to each other."

"And we'll send each other pictures ..."

"Of my new English boyfriend," Scarlett said devilishly.

Clem laughed. "And my movie star sweetheart," Clem finished.

Scarlett chuckled and gave Clem a hug. "Duh," she said, taking off her shoes and replacing them with her purple fuzzy slippers. "We have that new movie you wanted to see downstairs. Come on, I'll get it if you'll pop the popcorn."

"I don't believe it," Mrs. Greenly said for the thousandth time. "The stars of *The Truth Told by Me*? It's not possible."

Clem had already told her mother about the money she spent and, as Clem expected, her mom blew a gasket. She squawked at Clem for about twenty minutes about responsibility and all the things that Clem had already heard a million times. The only thing that bothered Clem about it was that Beverly was standing by, smirking at every word that came out of her mother's mouth. Now it was Clem's turn to smirk.

"You're lying," Beverly said, pushing up her seven sparkly bracelets that she had retrieved from her dress-up kit. She pushed her white, wide-brimmed hat (matching her flowing, fake, white feather boa) up out of her eyes as she looked at Clem's picture of the Clavis family.

"Beverly! You said you were going to get my pudding for me!" Brooke complained, stomping into the kitchen.

Clem looked at her. "Well, hello, Brooke. It's nice of you to join us while we are looking at the picture of my foreign exchange family," she said, grinning broadly.

"Brooke, I told you no more pudding for experiments! Those are for *lunches*," Mrs. Greenly said.

Emily E. Shipp

"But Mom! I'm so close to relating salmonella poisoning with pudding. I'll win the blue ribbon at the science fair for sure!" she said desperately.

Mrs. Greenly shook her head. "No."

"But *Mom* ..."—

"Just come over here and look at this picture! I can't believe Bailey didn't tell me about it!" Beverly bellowed.

Brooke obeyed and shuffled over to the three already sitting at the table. She gasped. "Huhhh!" She sucked in her breath. "It's that guy you love!" Brooke said, pointing.

Clem rolled her eyes. "I don't *love* him, okay?" Clem said, exasperated, knowing that actually this was a lie.

"Then how come you write him letters every week?" Beverly asked in a smart-aleck way. Clem pursed her lips and didn't answer.

"Can you believe that Bailey knew all along and never told us?" Beverly went on, waving her arms around. "Really. What is the point of being a triplet when you can't even collect secrets about your annoying older sister?" she asked.

Clem twisted her face up and gave Beverly a sour look. "Oh, I'm annoying? Then you must be looking in a mirror because the only annoying person I see around here is you," Clem shot back.

"Girls! Girls, please," Mrs. Greenly said, handing the picture back to Clem. "Stop acting like that. I already have two two-year-olds in the house." She got up and took out a pitcher of iced tea from the refrigerator.

"She started it," Beverly said.

Clem widened her eyes. "Beverly! Do you have to say that every time? It's so annoying!" she huffed bitterly.

Beverly stuck up her nose and flicked her boa up in the air. "If you'll excuse me, I have business to attend to." She waved her hand airily.

The Lopsided Miracle

Clem rolled her eyes and watched her younger, obnoxious sister stroll out of the room. "Mom, why can't we just send her off to a boarding school that specializes in prissy attitudes?" Clem said sarcastically.

Mrs. Greenly chuckled and poured the iced tea into her cup. "Sweetie, she's eight," Mrs. Greenly said, as if that explained everything.

"Hey!" Brooke said, offended.

"Never mind, Brooke. Just go upstairs and find something else to use for your salmonella experiment," Mrs. Greenly said. Brooke gave an exaggerated sigh and shuffled out of the kitchen.

Clem looked at her mother. "Eight-year-olds can be so ..."

"Childish?"

"Yes." Clem decided that was the perfect word to describe her sisters—well, Brooke and Beverly anyway—childish.

"That's because they *are* children," Mrs. Greenly explained. "They have the right to act like eight-year olds." She took a sip of her drink and looked her daughter square in the eye. "I remember when you were little. So full of curiosity and wonder..."

"Oh Mom, please. Not 'The Wonder Years'," Clem begged, rubbing her forehead.

Mrs. Greenly paused and then took another drink of her tea. "I'm just saying..." She set down her glass. "That then, you would have gone on that trip, fear or no fear of traveling, celebrity or no celebrity."

Clem opened her mouth to speak, but then shut it again. What did her mother mean? She decided to brush it off, maybe store it in the back of her head for later use, if it ever made any sense.

"Right Mom, but there *is* a celebrity ... no, two ... and I would've gone anyway for Scarlett," she said, shrugging. She began to walk out of the room when she heard her mother's last words.

"Would you have gone?"

~

Emily E. Shipp

"Wake up! Rise and shine! It's Christmas yet again!" Ben heard a voice from somewhere. He opened an eye slowly just to see where it was coming from, and he came face-to-face with a video camera.

"Ah!" he yelped, jumping up. He took a frazzled glance at who was behind the camera and then calmed down once he saw who it was—a laughing Jodie.

"Oh, my *God*!" Jodie exclaimed, laughing in fits. "You have to see your face on this thing! You would've thought you'd seen a ghost or something!"

Ben, in a rage, grabbed the camera out of his sister's hands. "Jodie. I'm going to kill you," he said, rewinding it a bit and playing the tape. He saw himself jumping out of sleep and grabbing the camera while Jodie was giggling in the background.

"You can't kill me," Jodie said, "for two reasons. One, I have a good lawyer who could whip the pants off of your scrawny little butt, and *two* ..." She paused at this. "It's Christmas!" She whipped out a present from behind her back.

Ben, in spite of his sister's rude intention, smiled. "Awww ... for me?" he asked sarcastically.

"Be quiet," Jodie said, sitting on the foot of his bed while he unwrapped it. She was secretly delighted to know that he was pleased with the gift.

"Jodie!" he exclaimed. "This is great!" He didn't care if he sounded like a father talking to a daughter. After all, it was just Jodie.

"I thought you'd like it," Jodie said, smiling.

"I do." He looked up at her. "Thanks, Jode."

Jodie gave him a hug. "Anytime."

"Ben! Angel Muffin! Breakfast!" Mr. Clavis called upstairs, knowing that at his words, his daughter would growl. She did.

"That man ..." Jodie said, releasing herself from the hug. "Well, come on. It's another one of our famous blueberry pancake breakfasts." Jodie walked out while Ben stretched himself, admiring the new present

The Lopsided Miracle

from Jodie—a book of sheet music Three's No Crowd had written over the time they had been together. He knew that Jodie had been collecting the music for the past couple of months, and now he knew why.

It had a professional cover with a large, blown-up picture of the band that had obviously been taken by Jodie when they were posing for her the day that she said she was doing a report on them. Yeah, right. He was embarrassed to say that he had believed her. Ryan, Mark, and Ben were sitting on a picnic table, eating Skittles—a regular routine. Ryan was pretending to be a monkey with his hands over his eyes, while Mark was pretending to be a monkey with his hands over his mouth. Ben was laughing, his head tilted backwards. At the top, it read, "Three's No Crowd" in big, bold letters with the band members' names separated by commas underneath. At the bottom, it read, "Edited and produced by Jodie Clavis." He flipped over to the back cover, where there was a picture of the band doing the same pose, but it was taken so that you could only see their backs. He smiled.

"Thanks, Jodie," he whispered to himself. A couple minutes later, he heard Jodie calling from downstairs.

"You're welcome, already! Just come on!" Sometimes the two believed that they had ESP because at random times they felt they could read each other's minds.

"I'm coming!" he yelled. He shuffled across the room, walked through the door (Jodie hadn't bothered to close it), and slid down the banister. Jodie, who was waiting for him, had seen him sliding.

"How elementary can you be?" she asked. "That is the most juvenile habit I have ever witnessed."

"How would you know? You've never tried it." He brushed past her and swept into the kitchen, hearing her grumble behind him.

"Mornin'," he spoke into the kitchen. His father and mother were looking perfect, as usual.

"Merry Christmas, Ben!" Mrs. Clavis said, smiling broadly.

Emily E. Shipp

He smiled back. *I am allowed to act little today*, he remembered, *after all, it is Christmas*. "Merry Christmas, Mom," he said, plopping himself into a chair. He smelled the pancakes from the tabletop and just for a minute, he forgot about the complications in his life.

I wish all days could be like this, he thought, taking a bite.

After everyone had eaten and Mrs. Clavis had received all the Christmas morning phone calls from Ben's grandparents and other relatives, they all made their way into the living room and sat down around the beautiful, broad Christmas tree.

Jodie beamed. "I love this part," she said, rubbing her hands together.

Ben laughed. "You're so stupid," he said, shaking his head. Mr. Clavis was already under the Christmas tree, pulling out presents for everybody. Neither he nor his wife said anything about the mild name-calling because there was no way they could have stopped it.

"Here's one for ... Jodie," he said, waving it around. Jodie grabbed it and set it in front of herself, examining it.

"Ben ... Jodie ... Ben ... here you go ..." he said, handing out more and more gifts. Everyone had packages and were just looking at them. Jodie even shook one at her ear as she had done as an eight-year-old.

"Mom, can we just open them all at one time this year? I hate waiting for Ben to open his. He takes forever," Jodie complained dully.

Mrs. Clavis looked at her two teens and then grinned. "Okay, but just for my babies," she said, laughing. Mr. Clavis smiled, too.

Jodie smirked. "Yeah, yeah," she said, opening her first gift. Everyone else started opening presents, too.

Ben started to open one from Grandmother Clavis. Then he looked at another parcel under the tree that his dad obviously had not seen. It was a small, white envelope. Ben brought it out and examined it. It had his name on it, his address to the set of the show, and a stamp in the right corner. He looked on the left corner to see whom it was from.

The Lopsided Miracle

"Clem Greenly," it said.

He grimaced. *Great. Now she is spoiling my Christmas, too*, he thought. Ungratefully, he flipped it over and tore open the flap that held it shut. He brought out a card with two golden bells on the front with cursive letters spelling out "Merry Christmas" right above it. He opened it up and out fell a picture.

It was a girl—Clem, he guessed. She was sitting in a chair, her elbow propped up on the back of it, but you couldn't see her legs, just her face. Her face was fairly pale with slightly rosy cheeks and bright green eyes. Her brown hair was flowing over her shoulder, which was covered in a cream-colored turtleneck. Her hair was straight with soft curls at the bottom, and her hand was running through her hair. She was smiling; her teeth were as white as vanilla frosting on a birthday cake.

But he didn't seem to see these qualities. He just saw the fan that was going to ruin his life, like in middle school. He swallowed, thinking. But instead of throwing it away just then, he put it back in the envelope to throw away later. He wasn't going to let something that was happening in the future affect him now.

Yet January second was creeping up very, very soon ...

CHAPTER SEVEN

"Pass the stuffing, please," Grand-mama said politely to Clem.

Clem smiled. "Here you are, Grand-mama," she said politely back, taking the hot dish and handing it to her. It was the Greenly family tradition to have dinner on Christmas night with Mr. and Mrs. Greenly, all their children, and Mr. Greenly's parents. Mrs. Greenly's parents were dead.

"Such a well-mannered young woman," Grand-mama complimented. "Children," she directed her conversation to the rest of the Greenly children, "I hope you look up to your sister. Such a wonderful role model she is." Stephen made a face to Clem and Clem gave him a *what-can-I-say* look while sloshing her red cranberry juice softly around in her wine glass.

"Well, no. Let's not forget the other role model around here," Grand-papa reminded, pointing to Stephen.

Stephen smirked at Clem. Clem grimaced back. "Thanks, Gramps," he said, while Grand-papa gave him a fatherly pat on the back. Clem rolled her eyes, but she was pleased to know that Beverly was infuriated with all the attention being directed to her elder sister and brother.

They all had on their Christmas-wear and were sitting in the dining room, which was beautifully decorated with holly and mistletoe (although every kid refused to kiss anyone unless it was a parent), and eating on the finest Christmas china. Clem always thought that this was the best part of Christmas, because she loved her grandparents so much and only got to see them twice a year: Christmas, when they came to South Carolina, and Easter, when the Greenly family traveled to Texas to visit them.

Emily E. Shipp

The conversation shifted to everything *but* January second, when Clem would leave on a flight to Canada. She wished that they would talk about it so that she could brag about her celebrity hosts, but they had already talked about it when they were opening presents and obviously the grandparents found politics interesting and Clem's favorite subject, at that moment, boring.

So while Clem nibbled at her corn, she had to listen to *everything* the adults wanted to talk about. She entertained herself by thinking about her presents upstairs in her room that she would now have to pack into her luggage for Canada. She had received the usual—clothes (she guessed her mom hadn't understood that large quantity she had just bought), CDs, gift certificates, money, jewelry, picture frames, and candles. It was what she usually received for Christmas, but there was one thing that she was really grateful for, even more so than the other things. It was a picture of everyone else in her family—her mother, her father, the twins, the triplets, and Stephen—all wearing black turtlenecks, posing in a black background, but with a lighting so perfect that you really could only see their faces. They were all smiling—even the twins were smiling sweetly—and the whole thing was put in a wooden picture frame with the word "FAMILY" engraved at the top. Clem almost cried when she took it out of the pretty, red wrapping paper. She hadn't realized, since her shock about the host family in Canada, how much she was going to miss her family.

After dessert, when the table had been cleared, everyone said goodnight and headed to bed. Clem was so excited—in seven more days she would be living with Ben Clavis. The thought was so exhilarating she didn't think she could sleep. However, she ended up in a very heavy and long slumber.

The next morning was so embarrassing she wanted to go back to bed and sleep the rest of the day. She woke up and went (slid) downstairs for breakfast, like always. When she went around the corner into the kitchen, passing Stephen playing the piano (something he was

The Lopsided Miracle

trying to do to impress Chelsea), she saw her mother sitting on a stool at the island in the middle of the room. She was stirring her coffee with a spoon, making the creamer swirl. When Clem came in, she turned around and smiled at her.

"Hello, dear," she said, kissing Clem's forehead. "What would you like for breakfast?"

"Don't worry about it, Mom," Clem said, opening the pantry and retrieving some Yum-Yums cereal. "I'll make it. You've done nothing but cook since before last night's dinner."

Mrs. Greenly sighed. "Oh, thank you so much, Clem," she said. Once Clem's cereal was made, Mrs. Greenly patted the seat beside her. "Here, sit down. I have to talk to you about something."

Clem obeyed, clueless as to what was coming. She propped herself up on the stool and took a bite of cereal. Her mother began to talk.

"Now, don't think I don't trust you when I point this out, but your grandmother and I were talking last night and she brought up a very important issue that I have forgotten to remind you of... about the exchange program," she said. Clem stopped eating for a moment, thinking about what her grand-mama could have messed up now, with a mouth big enough for two tongues. Clem shrugged and started eating again, wondering what it was.

Stephen came in with Chelsea just then, but no one noticed their entrance.

"Now, I really wasn't expecting for you to go into a boy's house for this program. I'm still wondering why they put you in the same house with a boy very close to your age, but I think they put you there because there *is* a girl there, but all the same ..." She brushed a piece of hair away from her face. "I think it's time for 'the talk' again."

All of a sudden, there was a noise from across the kitchen. Stephen had spit out his orange juice and was laughing so hard his face was red. Chelsea had put her hand over her heart and stuck a smile on her face, as if Clem were the sweetest thing.

"Mom!" Clem whispered harshly. Mrs. Greenly looked at Clem and shook her head as if she had no idea that Clem was being embarrassed right before her very eyes. Chelsea walked over and put a hand on Clem's shoulder. Stephen was still laughing.

"Now, Clem," Chelsea started. "You shouldn't be ashamed of having this talk. It's very important for girls your age to understand these things."

"Right. It's important for our little baby to grow up about now," Stephen said, hooting hilariously.

"Stephen, hush," Chelsea said. "It's not her fault if she's naïve about these things."

"Ah!" Clem said, ripping away from Chelsea's grasp and running from the kitchen, her face beet red. She had never been so embarrassed in front of one of Stephen's girlfriends. Chelsea was over at Clem's house *all* the time! How could she face Chelsea now that she thought Clem was just a little, immature kid? She would never forgive her mother and certainly never her grand-mama for bringing it up in the first place! Clem barged into her room and shut the door securely before locking it so no one could get in. Then she threw herself on the bed and buried her head in a pillow.

This was *not* a good way to start off one of the last mornings she had with her family before she left!

She cooled off in minutes, but it took a lot of pillow punching and growling to pull it off. Even though she was calmed down, she still couldn't face Chelsea again—or not today, anyway. So she waited until she saw Chelsea's car pull out of the driveway before leaving her room. Sure, she was embarrassed, okay ... *very* embarrassed, but that didn't mean she couldn't enjoy the small amount of time she still had with her family. After all, she only had six days left.

The Lopsided Miracle

    The day finally arrived.

    Clem's suitcases were all stacked by the door. Her entire family was awake, in spite of the sleep they lost two nights before on New Year's eve. Clem was more excited then she had ever been in her entire life. Her plane departed at 5:00 A.M., so she had to leave for the airport at 3:30 so she could get there in time to get situated. Her whole family was sleepy, but Clem appreciated their waking up so that she could have one last look at them before she walked out the door.

    The triplets gave her a homemade card made from construction paper, sparkly art glue, and markers. On the front on the yellow card, it said, "We'll Miss You" and on the inside was a picture drawn of Beverly, Brooke, and Bailey all holding hands with each other with Clem in the middle. It was signed "The Three Muska-tears," since they didn't know how to spell musketeers. Her parents gave her a store-bought card with the same "We'll Miss You" message and a picture of Clem's house loosely placed inside. Stephen gave her a hug and a kiss (with a package of chocolate kisses—from both Stephen and Chelsea), and the twins each gave her hugs.

    Clem cried when she left the house, but her mother understood. Mrs. Greenly loaded up all of Clem's things in the minivan with all the bumper stickers. Then she backed out of the driveway, and Clem watched her house get farther and farther away until they rounded a corner and it was gone.

    Since it took an hour to reach the airport, Clem was able to catch up on some sleep, but she woke fifteen minutes before they were due to arrive so she could check her face and hair in the mirror. She had put her hair in a messy bun near the top of her head—the kind that cheerleaders wear so often—and picked a new, royal blue shirt with quarter-length sleeves to wear with her new low-rider bellbottoms. She wore the new, white tennis shoes she got for Christmas with comfortable socks. She had checked her face in the mirror to make sure there were no pimples and then applied lip liner, pink-colored lip-gloss, eyeliner,

Emily E. Shipp

and mascara. Clem's mother wanted to burst when she saw her fifteen-year-old wearing eyeliner and mascara. It looked great, and Clem didn't understand why she couldn't wear it now.

"Come on, Mom! I'm fifteen, for goodness sakes!" she argued.

Her mother sighed. "Oh, all right." She gave in. Clem was happy. She wanted to look good for Ben, after all.

When the duo finally reached the airport, Clem was more than happy to get out of the minivan. Her mother liked to have the air conditioning always bursting because of the hot weather, but Clem liked it hot. She guessed that she should get used to the cold, though.

Clem's mother couldn't seem to find any parking. No matter where she looked, empty spaces were either handicapped spots or fire zones. Time after time they would find a car pulling out, but then another car would pull into the space before they could get there. Just before Clem thought she would explode, they found a parking space. Unfortunately, it was in the very back of the lot, and Clem and Mrs. Greenly had to find a cart to lug all of Clem's things.

At last they reached the inside of the airport, and Mrs. Greenly helped Clem check all of her luggage. Once that was done, Clem was given her ticket and had to wait in a never-ending line to get her carry-on bag scanned to make sure that she wasn't carrying anything illegal. Clem hated this because there was a man in front of her who smelled strongly of mustard and whose fat hung over the sides of his belt—in fact, there was even fat hanging over his large, corny cowboy boots. Then there was a man behind her who wouldn't stop laughing. She didn't know what was so funny. The man was watching a baseball game.

"Strike one!" the television that hung from the ceiling in the waiting area called out. The man laughed.

Clem rolled her eyes and gritted her teeth. "Mom," she whispered, but her mother was too involved in *Martha Stewart Living* to pay attention.

The Lopsided Miracle

Finally, her bags were checked and she was through the gate. She turned around and peered into her mother's eyes. "I'll miss you," she said.

Her mother's eyes watered, and Clem noticed that her mother was obviously trying to fight back the tears. "I love you, Honey," she said, grabbing Clem into one last hug. Clem breathed in her mother's scent—fresh lilies mixed with a cinnamon smell.

"I love you, too, Mom," Clem said softly, closing her eyes.

After a few minutes, her mother let go. "Now, don't get yourself into any trouble and remember our talk," Mrs. Greenly said.

Clem smiled. This was the mother she was used to. "Don't worry, Mom." Clem kissed her mother's cheek. "I've got to go before the plane takes off without me. I love you," she said, waving and walking into the corridor.

"Bye!" her mother said, waving and smiling. Clem grinned and turned around. The corridor was dark and had cold air blasting into it. She took a deep breath, and then walked. She was walking into her future, and leaving the past behind.

For now, anyway.

~

"Ben! Come on! We're going to be late!" Jodie called, scurrying around like a mouse running from a broom. He was lying on his bed, trying not to think about anything. Now he had to think about it; he had no other choice. It was time.

"If we're two seconds late, I don't think she'll mind," Ben said, criticizing his mother and sister who were always on time for everything. Now, in particular, he wished that he could freeze time so that he could have more time to himself before Clem barged into his life.

"*I* would mind!" Jodie said, pulling on her coat over her sweater and wrapping a scarf around her neck. "If we're late, we'll be making a bad impression. Duh!"

Emily E. Shipp

I hope we make a bad impression. Then she'll go home, Ben thought miserably. He groaned and forced himself off the bed.

"Why do I have to come again?" Ben asked the air. Jodie heard him.

"Because, dumb-o!" Jodie said, opening the door. Ben heard the car already running and knew it would be warm when he came out. "You're the star of the show!"

Walking downstairs, he closed his eyes, wishing he could just die right then. Why did his life have to be so unfair?

He opened the door and looked out at the weather. Immediately, he jerked his head back in and shut the door, wiping snowflakes out of his eyes. It was a blizzard out there!

Maybe her flight was cancelled ... he started to think, but before he could think anymore, he was pulled out the door by Jodie, his coat in her hands.

"Jodie!" he yelled, snatching his coat away from her and bundling up inside it. "You little—"

"Don't even try me," Jodie said, racing to the car. "We're late!" Ben, still furious with his sister for pulling him out into a blizzard without a coat on, walked as slowly as he possibly could to the car, enjoying the annoyed look on Jodie's face. He watched as she rolled her eyes, turned to their mother, and said something. After about three seconds, the horn beeped loud and long. Ben would have just walked slower, but he was getting very cold, and he was only about two steps away from the car, anyway.

He opened the door and a blast of hot wind hit him in the face. It felt so good that he leapt into the car and slammed the door shut to keep the cold out.

"It's about time," Mrs. Clavis said, turning around and backing out of the snowy driveway.

The Lopsided Miracle

"Yeah, about time," Jodie mumbled from the backseat. Ben didn't say anything, knowing that if he started to say something mean to his sister, he would never stop.

The ride to the airport was a long and silent one. It had stopped snowing hard, but it was snowing lightly throughout the whole trip. Ben didn't even look at his sister, and Jodie didn't say one word to him, either. She was occupied with doing crossword puzzles, which Ben thought was the geekiest thing to do, but he made no comment about it—he just snorted disapprovingly.

Mrs. Clavis had all she could take of the silence, so she started singing songs. This was the only thing that Ben and Jodie agreed on during the whole trip.

"Mom," Ben said, "I just thank the good Lord that none of my friends are in here right now."

"Seriously," said Jodie, who had stopped doing her crosswords and had been cleaning out her nails, "that is the lamest thing to do."

"Now, now," Mrs. Clavis said, smiling. "You two used to love singing road trip songs!"

"Yeah, and I used to like Barney, too, Mom," Ben said, sighing and staring at the snow from his window.

Mrs. Clavis's face looked hurt. "Well, I'm sorry I don't know the words to some rock shenanigan," she said, scowling at the road and clutching the steering wheel tightly.

"I do," Jodie said, clueless. Ben rolled his eyes. Mrs. Clavis didn't say anything.

By the time they reached the airport, everyone was a little frustrated. Fortunately, parking was very easy to find—most people must have thought the blizzard had cancelled all flights. Jodie got the flowers that they had picked out for Clem and walked as far away from Ben as she possibly could. Ben did the same. Mrs. Clavis caught on and walked between them, but made sure that they stayed close to her.

"I wonder what she'll look like," Jodie said to her mom.

Emily E. Shipp

"I don't know," Mrs. Clavis replied.

I do, thought Ben. He hadn't shown anyone the picture of Clem. As far as he knew, he was the only person in Canada who knew what Clementine Greenly looked like. They kept walking until they reached the gate where Clem was supposed to arrive. Jodie held the flowers as though they were a baby, making sure not to hurt them. Ben looked straight at the gate as a woman opened the door to let the passengers out. Old people, young people, and parents with babies all exited the gate and greeted people or left for a different gate.

"Where is she?" Jodie asked.

"Just look for a young girl who is alone," Mrs. Clavis said. Jodie bit her lip and kept looking.

They must have waited there for fifteen minutes before the whole gate was cleared. They were still alone, looking for Clem.

"Oh, no," Jodie moaned. "Either we've lost her, or we're blind."

"Maybe she didn't come after all," Ben said hopefully.

Mrs. Clavis raised her eyebrow. "I think someone would have called if she had changed her mind," she said. They waited for another minute and when she hadn't appeared, Mrs. Clavis furrowed her brow. "All right, maybe we should ask that man over there." She walked towards a man standing a short distance away from them wearing a nametag that Ben couldn't read. Just as she was about to talk to him, a figure came out of the gate.

She was average height with long, brown hair and bright green eyes. She couldn't be mistaken. She walked over to Ben with a broad smile on her face—she was clearly excited.

"Hi," she said, not taking her eyes off Ben, "I'm Clem."

~

She couldn't believe it. She was standing in the presence of Ben Clavis—the TV star she had dreamed about all her life. There he was, not even two feet away from her.

The Lopsided Miracle

"Hi," he mumbled, turning around and heading towards the bathroom. Clem's eyes looked worried.

Oh, great, she thought, *what did I do?*

"Hey!" another voice said. Clem turned around and saw Ben's sister, Jodie, the co-star of Clem's favorite show.

"Hi!" Clem said, a little too enthusiastically.

Jodie didn't seem to notice. She handed Clem a beautiful bunch of daisies. "These are for you," Jodie said. "I hope you like ..."

"Huhh!" a girl gasped from a chair by the gate. "You're Felicity!" She was referring to the name of Jodie's character on the show. All of a sudden, Clem felt foolish—like she was a little girl, too, being introduced to Brittany Spears.

Jodie laughed. "Yep, that's me," she said, smiling at the short ten-year-old.

"I love your show! It's my favorite!" she said, her eyes shimmering.

"Well, thank you very much!" Jodie said, looking down at the pen and paper in the little girl's hands. "Would you like me to sign an autograph for you?"

The girl nodded her head vigorously. "Oh, yes! Please!" She held the pen and paper up to Jodie's face. Jodie took the pen and paper and signed a quick signature.

Clem watched it all. She was so envious of Jodie for being able to just walk into an airport and have total strangers come up to her, praising her like a queen.

Mrs. Clavis was watching Clem the whole time, reading her thoughts. "It's not that great," she said to Clem. "We can't even go to the grocery store together anymore, especially not with Ben."

Clem smiled weakly.

"That must be tough," she said, sticking out her hand. "I'm Clem. You must be Mrs. Clavis."

Emily E. Shipp

"I am," she said. She shook Clem's hand. "Well, we must be getting your bags, and you might want to slip on a coat. It's a bit chilly outside."

CHAPTER EIGHT

"Cold?"

Clem looked at Jodie. "K-kinda," she choked out, sitting on the freezing leather seats of the car.

"Don't worry," Jodie laughed. "We can turn the heat up. Mom?" She gave her mom a look.

"No, please! If it gets any hotter in here then I'll start seeing ice cream stands in the snow," Ben said. Clem laughed in spite of her frigid body. The coat she had brought did not even start to compete with the cold.

"Sorry it's so cold. I guess you've never been this far north?" Jodie asked.

Clem shook her head. It was hard to move it. "No. The farthest I've ever gone north is to North Carolina, and that was southern North Carolina," Clem said.

"Really? That's funny. The farthest south I've ever gone is northern Michigan."

Clem smiled. "I bet you're happy you're used to the cold," Clem said.

Ben rolled his eyes. "Duh," he said.

Mrs. Clavis glared at him and then smiled sweetly at their guest. "Ignore whatever he says, Clem." She shifted gears in the car. "You don't mind if I call you Clem, do you?"

"No," Clem said, "not at all. Actually, I like to be called Clem." *This is pathetic,* she told herself, *you're making small talk with their mother!*

"Wonderful," Mrs. Clavis said, driving along the snowy roads. Clem looked at Ben, praying he would make conversation with her, but she had no such luck. Clem noticed that Jodie caught her staring at Ben, so Clem quickly moved her gaze from Ben to the window. The scenery was beautiful. Smooth snow covered everything, from the bare trees to the icy grounds. She looked down at the flowers in her lap. A question popped in her mind: *How in the world do people grow gardens around here?*

"Pretty, isn't it?" Jodie said.

Clem nodded. "I've never seen so much snow before," she said, eyes wide to the crystal-like flakes on the ground.

"Yeah. It's really fun. When Ben and I were little, we used to go sledding." Ben grunted. Jodie said loudly, "Sometimes I still go by myself, but Mr. I'm-too-good-for-everything never goes with me anymore."

Clem chuckled. "Sledding? Are you kidding? There are *seventeen*-year-olds in South Carolina who would die for a ride down a snowy hill. Half of the people there have never seen a snowflake in their lives," Clem informed them.

"Like you?" Jodie guessed.

Clem blushed. She didn't know why she felt embarrassed to say that she'd never seen snow before. She felt so ... inexperienced. "Yeah," Clem said, "like me."

On the journey back to the Clavises' home, Clem had made observations. Jodie seemed very nice and very polite, and Mrs. Clavis was the same way, but she liked to ask questions. The only thing she was worried about so far was Ben. He had only said about three words to her since she arrived and seemed to have no interest in speaking more. Was it something *she* had said? But how could that be? She had hardly said anything to him! Was there a piece of hair that stuck out of her head like a jack-in-the-box that no one had told her about? She wanted him to like her ... but how could he not like her when she had barely even introduced herself?

Jodie must have noticed that Clem was deep in thought, because she jested, "You're not thinking about going home already, are you?" and then smiled to prove it was a joke. Clem smiled, too. If Ben didn't like her, at least Jodie did.

The Lopsided Miracle

Later, they reached the subdivision where the Clavises lived. Clem probably wouldn't have noticed because she had been gawking at Ben's head, but Jodie announced it when the time came.

"Look out the window, Clem," Jodie said, pointing to a pretty stone sign with pine trees on either side. It read "Quinn Creek" in beautiful letters. Beyond the road leading them in were fountains. Clem supposed that they were beautiful when the water was turned on, but she couldn't tell because the fountains were iced over. Mrs. Clavis drove right past it. Clem looked around. Where she had lived, there was a golf course behind the fence of their large, beautiful, gated community. She hadn't known what to expect, but she had guessed that they lived in a more ... grand subdivision. Not that where they lived wasn't grand; actually, it was very upscale, with neatly cut lawns (Clem couldn't really see the lawns under the snow, but she guessed that they were all neatly cut), and all the houses were fairly large and cozy with wreaths on the doors. The very first thought that came to her mind when she passed it all was "family."

"Do you like it?" Jodie asked.

Clem nodded her head. "I love it. It's ..." She came very close to saying that it was very different from her old neighborhood, but she didn't know if they would take it as a compliment or an insult. "Lovely," Clem ended. She questioned herself on her use of the word "lovely" but before she could judge whether this was stupid or classy, the car, which was going over a small bump into a driveway, rocked her. The next thing she knew, the engine was turned off (along with the heating—to everyone's despair), and Mrs. Clavis had turned around and said, "Welcome home."

~

Ben coughed a little too loudly as he made his way out of the car and shut the door loudly, making sure his mother knew he was miffed at the whole deal. She just stared at him with a blank expression on her

Emily E. Shipp

face. Her pretty, deep blue eyes gave him a look of warning. *Don't even try to make her feel bad.*

"Let me help you with your bags," Jodie offered, interrupting his thoughts.

"Thanks," Clem said, "I'll need it."

What does she think she's doing? Ben thought. *It's like she's taking over. Talking to my sister like she's known her all her life.*

"After we put your stuff away, I'll take you on a tour of the house, okay?" Jodie said, making it sound like an option, even though Ben could tell she didn't really want it to be.

"Sounds great," Clem said. *She's so comfortable here*, Ben thought, *but she shouldn't be. She doesn't belong here.*

Ben opened the door and breathed in the deep scent of chocolate. He knew his dad was making something. He took off his coat and shoes and threw them carelessly on the floor. If anything, maybe Clem would leave because the house was so disorganized. *No*, he thought, *that's stupid. Mom keeps this place as clean as her best china.* He quickly put his shoes away and hung his coat on the bar in the coat closet. Slumping, he shuffled to the kitchen where the chocolate smell grew stronger.

Sure enough, he found his dad hunched over a cookbook, which was placed on the kitchen counter. Ben hopped up beside it, looking at the heading of the page his father was reading. It said, "Chicken and mandarin pot pie."

"Sounds nasty," Ben said.

"Yeah," Mr. Clavis said, "well, it's not really a pot pie. It's more like ... a soufflé."

"With mandarins?" Ben asked.

Mr. Clavis shut the book. "Never mind. I'm making cake right now, anyway." Ben jumped back down off the counter and followed his dad to the oven.

"Why? You never make cake," Ben said.

The Lopsided Miracle

Mr. Clavis opened and closed the oven door, letting the most delicious whiff of chocolate cake out into the kitchen. "Because we have a guest." He smiled. Ben didn't even try to look happy. Mr. Clavis gave him a look. "What?" he asked. "Is there something wrong with her?"

"No," Ben sighed. "I just ..." He looked at his dad. Ben could tell that he was thrilled to have a guest in the house. Ben wanted to make Clem have a miserable time, so she would leave and let everyone get back to normal again, but he didn't want to make his family miserable, too. Yet, if everyone loved Clem and she left, wouldn't that make his family miserable?

"Nothing," Ben said, utterly confusing himself. "Never mind."

"Oh, well, okay," Mr. Clavis said, "but if you ever need to talk about anything, you know I'm here."

Ben nodded. "Yeah, okay." He distracted himself by counting the pots and pans hanging from the ceiling over the island before his mother came in and started talking to him.

"Ben? Will you be a dear and go get your sister and Clem for dessert?" She kissed Ben on the head. Ben felt like he was in an old black-and-white movie.

"Can't you go get them?" Ben asked dully. Mrs. Clavis didn't even look back at him. He was desperate. "Dad?" he asked. Mr. Clavis cleared his throat, but then said nothing, catching on to his wife's intention. Ben threw his head back, sighed, turned around, and shuffled out of the kitchen.

He had to drag himself upstairs. He could hear his sister and Clem in Clem's new room putting her things away. He couldn't really tell what they were saying, but sometimes he caught a fragment of a sentence like "... so heavy ..." and "thanks a lot ... really appreciate it." For some reason, this made Ben mad. Why was Jodie so happy with Clem? He knew he was being unreasonable. Because he was angry about Clem's arrival, he wanted everyone else to be angry, too, but he couldn't help it. He told himself that it was his nature to be mad at Jodie

Emily E. Shipp

for having a great time when he was wallowing in depression. Yet deep down, he knew that he was just being selfish, though he didn't want to admit it.

He knocked once on the door, hoping that no one would hear him. Unluckily, Jodie did.

"What?" she called, laughing at something Clem had said.

"Dessert," he mumbled.

"Oh," she said.

Well, Ben thought, *at least the conversation is the same.* Clem opened the door. She obviously wasn't expecting Ben to be there, because when she saw him, she widened her eyes and started pushing hair back behind her ears. Ben wanted to say something like, "Don't even try to impress me. It's never going to work," but he didn't. He just stayed silent, turned around, and walked back down the steps before Clem could say anything.

When he got back downstairs, he had to smile because the cake had come out of the oven. He wished that Mark, the chocolate lover, were there to help him eat his slice. He didn't feel like eating. Finally Clem and Jodie reached the kitchen, and it was then that Ben made up his mind.

"Mom, can I go to Ryan's?" he asked, standing up and turning his back to the foreign person standing in the same kitchen he had eaten in since he was born.

"Ben ..." Mrs. Clavis looked at him and then stole a glance at Clem.

Ben just headed for the garage, where his car was parked. "Thanks. I'll be back by dinner," he said and then shut the garage door, knowing that since it was still pretty early in the day, he would have all afternoon to talk to Ryan. He hurried toward his car and then remembered that his keys were in his coat pocket. Quickly, he walked around the house in his socks and T-shirt, opened the front door silently, and grabbed his coat and keys from the closet. His socks were wet

The Lopsided Miracle

from walking in snow on the way to the front door, so he took a pair of big boots and tugged them on before closing the door again. He went back to the garage and started up his clean, orange car. He needed a getaway, and he hoped Ryan could help him.

~

Clem shoved some more cake into her mouth. She didn't notice that she was shoveling it rudely until she noticed how poised Jodie was when eating. She immediately straightened her back and reached for her napkin to wipe the corners of her mouth.

"I hope you like it here," Mr. Clavis said, smiling. "It's very nice here in Canada. Cold, but hey, that's why they invented furnaces!" he joked. Clem grinned, too. She really liked Mr. Clavis. He hardly asked her any questions and just liked to brag about how fabulous everything was. Some people may have considered this impolite, but to Clem, it made him seem more fatherly. Suddenly, Clem felt homesick for her own father—but the feeling only lasted a second, because she knew that she could always call him.

"How was the weather in South Carolina?" Mrs. Clavis asked.

Clem shrugged. "It was okay. We had some cold weather, believe it or not. It's pretty warm throughout most of the year, but it's cold in the winter." Clem looked out the wide kitchen window. "Just not as cold as it is here."

For some reason, Jodie found this funny, and started laughing. Clem looked sideways at her. "What's so funny?" she asked, feeling the ends of her mouth begin to turn up also.

Jodie shook her head and managed to swallow the chunk of cake that was in her mouth. "Nothing," she said, pulling down the sleeve of her turtleneck over her thumbs. "I'm done with cake. What about you?" She looked at Clem. Clem took the last bite of cake, leaving just a bit of frosting on the plate along with a few crumbs. She nodded, chewing up the portion in her mouth.

Emily E. Shipp

"That's probably a good idea. To finish unpacking, I mean," Mr. Clavis said, collecting the plates while Mrs. Clavis retrieved the glasses, which had been filled with milk.

Jodie looked at Clem. "Let's go back upstairs. You'll probably want to get all that stuff unpacked tonight. It'll probably feel good to you." Pushing back her chair, Jodie waited for Clem to get up. Once they were out of the kitchen, Jodie started talking.

"Well, I've told you all about my family—Ben ..." She rolled her eyes at this. "And everything. But you haven't really told me anything." They reached the steps.

Clem clutched the banister. "Do you really want to hear about my family?" Clem asked. Jodie nodded. Clem sighed, "Okay. But, it may take a while." They walked into Clem's room. Somehow, though, it didn't feel like home yet. It was still ... different. And it had a different smell, too. It wasn't a bad new smell, just different. While Clem's old house had smelled of Lysol, Jodie and Ben's house smelled like pine trees and holly berries. It was wonderfully refreshing.

So far, to make Clem's room feel like Clem's room, they had unloaded all of her shirts and sweaters, socks, and other under-things (Clem had done all of those) into the bureau. Then they had hung up all of her pants and jackets in the closet, and put her shoes on the closet floor (Jodie did that). Then, they had put her scarves, hats, etc. into the bureau too, in the extra drawer. Since Clem had brought an extremely large quantity of clothing, this task had taken them a long time. When Jodie opened the bedroom door, they remembered their hard work.

"It doesn't look like we've done anything," Clem remarked.

"Yeah, but we did get your clothes put away, finally." She smiled.

Clem chuckled. "Thanks again, so much, for doing this with me," she said, heading over to another one of her suitcases.

"Oh, it's no problem!" Jodie said, following her. "After all, I want us to be friends."

The Lopsided Miracle

All of a sudden, Clem looked up. Jodie was looking toward the suitcases, but Clem was a little surprised. Friends? She knew she shouldn't be surprised. After all, they were both fifteen and seemed to feel comfortable around each other, but it just seemed so shocking. She wasn't just talking about any regular teenager, but Jodie Clavis, a television star! Clem thought that Jodie would have so many friends she wouldn't even have room for another!

Jodie looked up and noticed Clem staring. Clem tried to hide her expression right away, but it was too late.

"What's wrong?" Jodie asked, thinking. "Was it something I said?"

Clem tried to busy herself by unzipping a lumpy case, but she had to say something. "Well, kind of," she said, looking up again. "It's just ... I want to be friends ..." She observed the puzzled look on Jodie's face. "Okay. It's just that ... you're Jodie Clavis, and I'm ..."

Jodie held her hand up in a "stop" motion. "I know what you're thinking," she said, "but let me tell you something right now. On Internet interviews and in the newspaper and on television I am Jodie Clavis. But around here, at home, around town, even in school, I'm just ..." She shrugged. "Jodie." It took Clem a little time to process this, but finally she got the message.

She didn't have to say anything, because Jodie went on, "I just want you to know that when you look at me, I don't want you to think, 'Oh, look. That's the TV star.' I want you to think, 'Hey! There's Jodie! The one who goes to a regular high school, lives in a regular house, and has a regular, annoying older brother.' No matter what, I will never stop being me. Even if I land the biggest, best job on Broadway, I will never stop being me—Jodie."

Clem felt like she was in a scene from a movie. Even the air in the room was intense and true. Clem couldn't talk, for fear of having something stupid and squeaky come out. But then, out of the blue, Jodie laughed. It broke the silence, and the only sound was Jodie's

Emily E. Shipp

ringing giggles. She doubled over with laughter. Her lip curled up so far that you could see a good portion of her pink gums above her teeth. Just the sight of her made Clem start laughing, too.

For some reason, it was then that she knew. She knew that she was going to be okay in Canada, because she would have Jodie as a friend. And soon, she would have new friends from her new school. *And sooner or later*, she dreamed, *I'll have Ben.*

CHAPTER NINE

"This is so retarded," Ryan said, getting into Ben's car. He was in his long pajama pants and an oversized T-shirt. Even though it was one o'clock, Ryan had woken up just fifteen minutes ago. Ben had driven over to escape his household.

"Sorry," Ben said, shifting gears and backing out of Ryan's driveway. "I need to talk."

"Oh, God, what now?" Ryan rubbed the bridge of his nose and sat down further in the passenger seat, mussing his hair even more.

Ben started driving down the street. "Put your seatbelt on," Ben said. "If I start talking, I might drive us off the road."

Ryan clucked his tongue, but didn't obey Ben's command.

"How bad is she?" he asked. "I mean, I'm just assuming that this was the day that you picked up your little houseguest." He closed his eyes and tried to fall back asleep in the seat.

"Wake up, you idiot. I need to talk to you." Ben snapped in Ryan's face.

Ryan snorted and swallowed a bunch of mucus. "Well, I'm listening," he said, opening his eyes halfway and scratching his head.

Ben sighed deeply. "She came," was all he could get out at first, but then once he found the words, they all flowed out. "She was just like I had expected. She was such a ... fan. I mean, whenever she sees me, she goes totally in 'flirt mode'. That's, like, the complete opposite of what I want. What anyone wants, really." He stopped at a red light. Ben was just wandering; he didn't really know where he was going.

"I just know I won't like her. I mean ... I don't like her. I haven't really talked to her, though, but I don't need to. I know she'll just be like all the other fans. You know, the stereotype kind of thing." He turned, passing a laundromat.

Emily E. Shipp

"She gets along with everyone, though. I mean, my mom loves her. Clem, that girl, was totally sucking up. It was disgusting. I knew I didn't like her, especially when she came up to me first when she got off the plane." He passed the mall, thinking vaguely about going in, but then decided against it.

"Then there's Jodie. Jodie acts like Clem is her new best friend, which is totally a lie. Jodie already has a best friend. I don't know who it is, but I know she must have one. My life would really, *really* be ruined if Clem became her best friend. But I don't have to worry because that will never happen. Right? Right." Ben made a sharp turn around a corner.

"My dad made this cake for her, too. He never makes cake anymore. He always thinks that we need all this healthy crap, but no. Today he made cake. It's like this girl has totally transformed my life. It's upside-down! But that's not the worst part. I'm talking about school. Remember how I told you about that girl in the seventh grade? Yeah, well, I can just tell this girl is going to be like that. Not as dramatic, but I am just hoping that she won't be too embarrassing. Thank God she's not in our grade." He put pressure to the pedal and zoomed across the road.

"I really don't know what to do. You'll have to see her. She even looks like a fan! It's horrible. What am I going to do? Huh? What am I supposed to do? I need her to go home. I want her to go home. She *needs* to go home. Am I right?" He swiveled his head to face Ryan, waiting for him to answer.

But Ryan couldn't. He was fast asleep.

~

"I'm home," Clem heard from her room. Her heart beat as fast as rabbits running. Ben was home again.

She was about to say hello, but then decided that that would be very childish. So she didn't say anything and continued to put her little trinkets on top of her pieces of new furniture. She heard footsteps

The Lopsided Miracle

coming up the stairs. She stopped suddenly and stared at her frosty white beanbag chair sitting in the corner. She heard the footsteps come closer to her room. She caught her breath in her chest, but then let it go once she heard the door to Ben's room open and shut again. Ben's room was two doors away from hers. A bathroom separated their rooms—the bathroom they now had to share. Clem was happy about this, but Ben was just depressed. Clem could see it in his eyes whenever he glanced at the bathroom door.

She was so deep in thought that she almost didn't notice the new figure she was about to put on top of her bureau. All of a sudden, she was distracted from Ben when she saw the glass jar with a copper, screw-on lid. It wasn't the jar that interested her, though. It was what was inside. The jar was filled with acorns.

Clem fought back tears, reading the little card taped to it. It had a picture of Big Ben, the famous clock tower, on the front. Inside, in black pen, was writing.

Clem,

I haven't left for London yet, but when you are reading this, I will probably be meeting my new "family" in this different place. I wanted to give you this jar of acorns to remember me by while you are in Canada, because when we were little, we used to play with them all the time. Remember? Mr. Acorn met Mrs. Acorn, and then they got married and had Baby Acorn ... I can still remember the look on your face when that little house you made for them got lost at the park. You were so sad, but still—we had wonderful times, and I hope that you'll put this somewhere where you can see it all the time and remember me forever. Remember to send me tons of pictures!

Hugs,
Scarlett

Emily E. Shipp

Clem wiped her tears away as she read the sweet card. She felt guilty for not thinking of giving something to Scarlett as Scarlett had done for her—but Clem hoped that she would remember her anyway, and somehow, she knew she would.

There was a knock on the door. It was so sudden that Clem jumped a bit, but then felt foolish for doing so. She turned around, hoping it was Ben, but no such luck. It was Jodie. She smiled.

"Did I scare you?" she asked, opening the door wider.

"No," Clem lied, hurriedly putting the jar of acorns in her bag. For some reason, she didn't feel she could share her acorn memory with Jodie, even though she was so extremely nice.

"I just wanted to show you where all of your toiletries go—where Ben can't mess them up," Jodie said, opening a door that led to the bathroom from Clem's room. Clem bustled around, trying to find her pack full of her toiletries, and finally, she found it. It was a big plastic case, meant for bathroom essentials, and it was white-and-blue striped with thin green lines and scattered purple dots.

"Okay," Clem said, following Jodie into the bathroom. Clem tried to flick on a light, but it was covered by the open door. Jodie found it first and turned it on.

"Okay, this is your cabinet," Jodie pointed out. It was a large, white, wall cabinet with a silver knob. Clem opened it and saw that there were three shelves—all empty.

"Sorry you can't have your own bathroom, but the spare one is in the basement, and we didn't think you would want to go all that way just to do something like brush your teeth," Jodie said. Clem nodded her head and put her bag on one of the shelves.

"You could have shared my bathroom, too," Jodie said, looking at the ceiling and then at Clem, "but it's already so full that you wouldn't even have been able to walk in there without losing something or stepping on something."

The Lopsided Miracle

Clem laughed, even though this wasn't supposed to be a joke. "It's that bad?" Clem asked. "Prove it."

Jodie widened her eyes and then shook her head. "All right, but if you get nauseous at any time, please tell me." She turned around and walked out of the bathroom, letting Clem turn the light off as she walked out.

They walked to the other end of the hall where Jodie's room was located. Jodie kicked open the door. It looked like any other teenage girl's room—full of magazines and posters and other things. Clem hardly even had time to glance at the desk that was covered with nail polish bottles before she was tugged into the bathroom. Jodie turned on the light. Clem bit her lip.

The room was just as Jodie had described it. You couldn't even see the floor except for a path that Clem supposed Jodie used each morning. The floor was covered with empty bottles of shampoo, nail polish (Clem supposed that Jodie really liked to use nail polish), face wash, old tissues, cotton balls, hair bands, bobby pins, and who knew what else. The shower curtain was wide open, revealing the inside of the shower, which was filled with different kind of conditioners, body washes, and so on. The sink was covered with makeup, makeup, and more makeup. The only thing that Clem could see clearly was the toilet.

"Ain't she a beauty?" Jodie said sarcastically.

This time, Clem really did laugh. "Oh, yeah," Clem said, raising her eyebrows. Jodie turned the light off and walked out of the messy area. Clem followed, making sure nothing had stuck to her feet.

"Well, my parents are always telling me to clean it up, but I mean, come on. I have to have my personality showing through somehow," Jodie said, sitting on her bed. For a minute, Clem didn't know what to do. She could sit down with her, but then she would feel like she was intruding somehow. If she just stood there, she would look like a freak. Jodie didn't seem to notice Clem's uneasiness though. Jodie got up and

Emily E. Shipp

sat down at her nail polish desk, motioning for Clem to sit on her bed. Clem did so, trying to act smooth.

After a few moments of silence, Jodie spoke up. "Do you want to see my new outfit for the first day back at school?"

Clem's nerves shivered. Jodie's words still rang in her head—*After all, I want us to be friends.* "Sure," she said, keeping her word about trying to know Jodie as Jodie, and not as a television star.

"Okay," Jodie said, hopping up and walking over to her closet doors, which were covered with pictures. While Jodie was digging through her messy closet, Clem took a closer look at the photos. One door was covered with photos of what looked like camp memories, photos of family and friends, and other normal pictures. The other door was full of pictures of the set of *The Truth Told by Me*, the other members of the cast, and Jodie with other movie stars she had met over the years. Clem's favorite picture, though, was a picture of Ben. He was wearing swim trunks and no shirt, and his hair was wet and messy—as if he had just dived into the water and then gotten out again. He was standing on a dock with the blue-green water of a lake in the background. He was smiling broadly (something, Clem regretted to say, that she had not seen so far), and it looked like a recent picture. She almost fainted when she saw it, and then silently rejoiced that she was living in the same household as a person who looked like a replica of the perfect Calvin Klein model.

"Here it is!" Jodie said from inside the closet. Clem leaned over to look inside, but Jodie was coming out, so they ran into each other.

"Oh! Sorry," they both said in unison. Then they started giggling.

"Oh, my God," Jodie said, rolling her eyes. "I'm so stupid. But anyway ..." She brought out the ensemble. It was a pair of dark blue bellbottom jeans that tied with brown lace and a brown midriff shirt with long, transparent sleeves that dipped low at the hands. It reminded Clem of the seventies with an Abercrombie and Fitch flair.

The Lopsided Miracle

"It's great!" Clem said, her voice going so high that she squeaked. Jodie just laughed again. *Calm down!* Clem tried to command herself, but it was impossible. So what if Jodie was a teenager—she was a teenager with fame!

"But the best part is I have new shoes to go with it." She hung her outfit back up and brought out the shoes—brown, strappy things with high, clunky heels.

"Awesome," Clem said, hiding her thumbs beneath her sleeves. This was reminding her that three days from now would be the first day of her new school—and she hadn't figured out what to wear yet. "Does the staff let you wear stuff like that?"

"Oh yeah," she said. "Well, actually, not really." Her smiled turned sneaky. "But that's one of the advantages of being on television—the teachers are suck-ups."

"Oh my! Jodie!" Clem said, covering her mouth so she didn't let any embarrassing sounds come out while she was laughing.

"Have you picked out anything yet?" Jodie asked. "I mean, for the first day of your new school?"

Clem shook her head. "I haven't had time. I mean, even at home I had a lot of stuff to worry about," Clem said.

"Well then, that's what we'll do," Jodie said. "And besides, you haven't told me about your family yet. We kind of wandered off subject when I asked you the first time."

"Okay," Clem said, walking to her new room, "but like I said before—it might take a while."

That night, after a dinner during which Ben said nothing to her but "pass the corn," Clem retired to her room. Almost everything was put away, except for a few little things that she had been too tired to put in place.

Emily E. Shipp

Jodie had said goodnight, and Mr. and Mrs. Clavis had said goodnight, but Ben had only grunted. Clem was exasperated. What was wrong with her? She wasn't *that* bad, was she?

She wrote all of this in the notebook that Chelsea, Stephen's girlfriend, had given her. It was just a normal, black-and-white splotched notebook, but it had a spiral binding. It was blank, and so Clem decided to write about the day that had started her six months in Canada. In the end, she filled up three pages—front and back. She closed it and put it in the drawer built into her bedside table.

Ben was ignoring her. He was hardly speaking to her, but the infuriating thing was that Clem had no idea why. Before she fell asleep, she made a promise to herself.

She was going to find out why.

~

Ben woke up the next morning feeling pretty good. He knew that he was going to be away all day—away from Clem. He was going to band practice, and he could show his friends his new music book that he had received from Jodie. He had told them about it, but they had yet to see it.

He got out of bed and walked into the bathroom. He still couldn't believe that he had to share a bathroom with a stranger. Not to mention a *girl* stranger. He noticed that the door from the bathroom that led into Clem's room was open. He reached out for the handle to close it, but before he could close it, his eyes caught sight of Clem.

She was lying in bed, her eyes closed and her hair still in a ponytail. Her comforter was hugged around her, and her mouth was slightly open.

Ben snorted and slammed the door shut. He didn't care if she woke up or not.

The Lopsided Miracle

"Marsha. What kind of a name is Marsha?" Ben asked, slamming the pack of Skittles down on the table in Ryan's garage. Ryan shrugged. "I can't believe he's ditching us for some girl named Marsha."

"You never know," Ryan said, pointing his finger. "*Mark* and *Marsha* might be a really *mighty* couple." His face was blank, but then once he realized how stupid he sounded, his face crinkled in a burst of laughter.

"Ryan, you get dumber by the day," Ben said with no hint of sarcasm. He didn't seem to get it.

"I know," Ryan said, still laughing.

Ben rolled his eyes. "Right ... Let's just try it without Mark," he said, pulling out his music.

"You know," Ryan said, putting his hand on Ben's shoulder, "I think we should just take today off. I mean, you need it bro."

Ben sighed. After a while, he picked up the pack of Skittles again and ripped it open. "Whatever," he said.

Ryan winked and snapped. "That's the spirit!" he said exaggeratedly.

Ben didn't say anything for a moment; he just shook his head. "You're an idiot," he said, smiling.

"Enough with the insults," Ryan said (loudly and in a fake Irish accent) and opened the door. "How about a little round of digital video entertainment, me lad?"

~

"So ... where's Ben?" Clem asked, trying to sound casual. Actually, she had been searching all day for him. Where could he be?

"Band practice," Jodie said, still looking at her magazine.

"Oh," but then she finally comprehended what Jodie said. "Oh, my God. He's in a band?" She sounded too excited when she asked this.

Emily E. Shipp

Jodie eyed her skeptically. "Yeah," she said slowly. "Is that a problem?"

"No, no," Clem said, getting control of her reactions. Even though she was calm on the outside, her insides were turning back flips. *He's in a band! That is so cool! Oh my gosh, I can't believe he's in a band! He really is perfect!*

"Do you have to go to the bathroom or something?" Jodie asked. "You seem really squirmy."

"No, that's okay. I guess ... I guess I'm just excited about school on Monday." *Oh Lord. What a lame excuse,* Clem thought.

Jodie just gave a short, sighing laugh. "Believe me, hun, my school is nothing special. It's really boring." She went on reading the magazine article. Clem wanted to say, "I know it's going to be boring! I just couldn't think of anything good to say," but that would have seemed really juvenile, and she didn't want to seem like a kid around Jodie. Instead, she got up and headed to the stairs. Maybe she could find something to do downstairs.

When she reached the steps, she realized that this was the first time she had been by herself in the house. The whole time she'd been there, Jodie or someone else (except for when she was using the bathroom and going to sleep) had escorted her.

She looked down at the railing. It was broad and smooth and long with no hard handle at the bottom—perfect for sliding. Before she could stop herself and think about how stupid it looked, she was on the railing, feet inward, and sliding down as fast as she could go.

Memories pounded in her head of when she slid down her home railing as a child. She landed perfectly on her feet, smiling happily—until she saw who was standing right at the front door.

Ben.

~

He had seen it all.

The Lopsided Miracle

He walked in the front door after having been over at Ryan's for what seemed like forever. He had thought he was having a very good day, but that one little sight ruined it all.

She had taken the habit.

His habit.

She was sliding down the railing he had slid down all his life. She seemed to be having a good time, too. He didn't think she even noticed him come in the door until he closed it shut and it creaked loudly. She whipped around and all the blood in her body seemed to rush to her face.

"Oh," she said, nervously tucking hair behind her ear and straightening her shirt. "Uh ... hey!"

"Hello," Ben said, glaring at her. She had taken a part of his life away. It was no longer his habit. The person he hated most at that moment shared it.

"Uh ... I'm sorry. It's like an old habit I have. I ... I couldn't resist. I'm sorry," she said, smiling weakly and then rocketing upstairs and into her room.

Ben was still scowling at the spot where she had been standing. He hated her. She was slowly taking away all the important things in his life.

Or that's what it felt like anyway.

He threw down his coat and felt like screaming. He clenched his fists and reminded himself that he was sixteen and just because something made him mad didn't mean he had to explode ... even though that was exactly what he felt like doing. *I knew I didn't like her*, he thought. *I just don't. I just want her to dissolve and disappear forever.*

He swallowed and made his way into the family room. He sat down stiffly and cleared his throat as if to make a speech in front of an invisible crowd, but he didn't say anything. He picked up his script on the table next to him and stared at the lines. He might as well do something productive to release his fury.

Emily E. Shipp

    His eyebrows furrowed. He shouldn't have to be angry in his own house. Home was supposed to be a peaceful place. *But no, nothing is ever easy for me,* Ben thought. *Nothing is ever easy for the great Ben Clavis.*

CHAPTER TEN

"Rise and shine! Good morning, Toronto. This is your number one, favorite radio station, 103.7 TREK, and we're going to play some of your absolute favorite music, first up …—" Clem switched the radio off. She rubbed her eyes and blinked a couple of times. It was finally here.

School was back in session.

She staggered out of bed, scratching her head and squinting through tired eyes. She and Jodie had stayed up until 10:30 deciding on her outfit for the first day at Jodie and Ben's high school. It felt as if Jodie and Clem were getting closer and closer by the minute. Clem couldn't be happier about her relationship with Jodie. Ben on the other hand …

Clem opened the bathroom door, just as she had every other morning, to take her shower, but when she did, puffy water vapor streamed out. Panic flooded her. Had she left something on? Was something burning? But then she realized it wasn't smoke at all. It was steam. She waved it away to see clearly, and she did. Ben was standing there in a towel, shaving his face.

"Ah!" she yelped. She jumped back, covered her face, and sprinted out. He nicked his face as he jumped in shock. He gasped as she closed the door. He was flustered. Had Clem just seen him standing in a towel? He was distracted from this thought by the little square of blood starting to form on his left cheek.

"Dammit," he whispered.

Clem, on the other hand, had shut the door and was gasping for breath on the outside of it. "Oh, my, gosh," she breathed. Her thoughts started to form clearly in her head. She had seen Ben Clavis … standing in the bathroom … in a towel … nothing but a towel …

She slowly smiled. Scarlett would *love* to hear about this.

Emily E. Shipp

She met Jodie at the breakfast table. Jodie had on the ensemble that she had shown Clem before, and with her hair and makeup done as Clem had never seen before, she looked fantastic.

"You look great," Clem said, sitting down beside her.

"Thanks," Jodie smiled. "Right back at cha." Clem was wearing gray, black, and white pinstriped pants, black boots, and a white blouse. Clem had straightened her hair so that it was straighter than a pin and fell over her shoulders pleasantly. As for her makeup, she was wearing brown eyeliner and clear, glassy lip-gloss. She was really glad she had bought it. "You can get some cereal if you want."

"Okay," Clem said, getting back up and heading over to the cabinet that she thought was the pantry. She was right. She grabbed the box of Frosted Wheat-O's and went to the refrigerator to get the milk. She didn't notice that Jodie was staring at her until she was walking over to sit back down at the table. Clem smiled.

"What? Do I have something on my face?" she asked, gesturing to her complexion.

Jodie clucked her tongue. "You are really pretty," she said.

Clem laughed. "No I'm not."

"Yes, you are. You have great model-like hair, perfectly straight teeth, and that outfit tops it off," Jodie proclaimed. "You'll knock 'em dead."

Clem was flattered, especially since these words were coming from a girl who had probably been a model once before and was plenty beautiful herself. Clem held her breath, hoping that Ben would think that same thing about her.

"Thanks," Clem said, not knowing what else to say. She took a few bites of cereal and then asked Jodie another question. "By the way, how are we getting to school?" Clem was used to riding the bus, but she didn't know how the school systems worked in Canada.

"We ride our bikes," Jodie said. Clem looked at her with wide eyes. Riding *bikes*? In *zero degree weather*? Clem gaped at Jodie, who

The Lopsided Miracle

at Clem's gaze, laughed. "I'm just kidding. My mom takes us, but she drops us off at the curb so it's not, like, embarrassing or anything." Clem smiled, relieved. She remembered her own mother and her car—the minivan with the bumper stickers.

Just then, Ben came into the kitchen, and Clem looked down at her cereal, turning a bright shade of scarlet. She could not get the vision of him wrapped in a towel out of her head.

"Morning, Ben," Jodie said.

"Mornin'," he replied.

Clem didn't say anything, but then remembered Jodie's compliment about how she looked and gained full confidence in herself. "Good morning," she said loud enough so that Ben could hear her. Ben turned his head, stared at her, then grunted and turned away. Clem raised her eyebrows.

Jodie huffed. "Honestly, Ben, you can't even say good morning to Clem? What, are you scared of her or something?" As soon as the words left Jodie's mouth, Clem wished that she hadn't said them. They were offensive somehow, and she didn't know how Ben was going to react. Ben sucked in a lot of air and then slammed the pantry door shut. Jodie jumped a bit.

He was clutching the bread so hard that Clem thought he was going to squeeze the bread right out of the bag. He marched right up to Clem and leaned down so that his nose was practically touching hers. In different circumstances, Clem would have loved to kiss those gorgeous, full lips right then and there, but of course, he was scowling at her. Besides, Jodie was in the room, and it would have been totally embarrassing.

Ben continued to stare at her, taking her eyes on a journey, searching them, but it wasn't a pleasant search. It was as if he was going to say, *Why are you here in the first place? Why don't you leave?* Maybe he was, but Clem never got to find out because he soon growled,

Emily E. Shipp

"Good morning," and then stomped away, not even putting the bread in the oven to toast.

Jodie rolled her eyes and put her hand on Clem's shoulder. "I'm so sorry about my brother. He's a real idiot," she said.

Clem swallowed. She should have been upset that Ben was being mean to her, but she couldn't help liking him. He was as hot as the sun, and she was sure that things would get better. They *had* to.

"Yeah," Clem said, "an idiot."

~

Ben parked his car in the middle of the school parking lot in his usual spot. He smiled when he saw his "posse" waiting for him.

"Hey man!" Ryan greeted, holding out his hand. Ben slapped it, and then they finished their handshake by snapping and rolling their shoulders, followed by other pointless movements. It was a stupid handshake they had had ever since Three's No Crowd had started. Mark was there, too, with a pretty blonde girl draped around him.

"Hey, babe," the girl said, smiling.

Ben noticed that her teeth were very straight, but very big. "Um, hello," he said. The girl giggled.

"Hey, dude. This is Marsha." Mark turned his head toward the girl. She giggled again. Ben found it very annoying.

"So," Ryan asked, "where's the exchange person?"

Ben groaned. "You'll see her around, but we're not talking to her. I hate her guts."

"Oh," Ryan said. Ryan decided not to ask why he hated her guts, because he didn't want to have another long speech like the one Ben had already given him in the car on vacation.

"Well, let's go inside," Ben said, looking at his school.

Ryan and Mark shrugged. "Okay," they both said.

Marsha smiled again. "I hate school," she put in. Ben shook his head. Why did she smile at everything?

The Lopsided Miracle

They all made their way into the school, occasionally being stopped by cheerleaders and other girls who had crushes on them (and their fame). Ben was trying to make his way to his locker before he was spotted by ...

"Oh, *my God*! *BEN*!! Oh *my gosh* I can't believe you're, like, here on the first day of school! I thought you would, like, sleep in or something, but you know how I can be totally wrong sometimes; I can't believe I thought that! Now I totally feel stupid! Oh my gosh ..."

It was Fiona Whitewaters—the girl who came the closest to his middle school nightmare. She had had the biggest crush on him ever since the day he walked into secondary school, and she was also quite popular. He didn't see how his peers could possibly choose such an unpleasant girl to be popular. She was always giggling from across the room when he sat down at lunch, starting up the most irritating conversations whenever he walked by, and asking him to every dance the secondary school had held. When he was still young and unknowing, he had said yes to one of her dance offers. After that, he never said yes again.

It had been the worst experience ever. She had spent the whole dance showing him off to her friends and giving them evil grins from across the dance floor. Also, she had wanted to dance to every song, and Ben hated dancing. So he ended up faking sickness and left early, thinking she would get the picture, but no. Ever since then she had been following him around like a lovesick puppy.

He pretended not to hear her while Ryan sort of nudged her out of the way. He knew all too well that Ben didn't exactly like her very much. She waved wildly and grinned broadly, yelling over Ryan and Mark's heads.

"Bye, Ben! See you later!" Then she walked off with her friends.

How about not, Ben thought, smiling at Marsha and Mark as they walked off together to class. Since Ryan's locker was right by his, they walked to their lockers together.

Emily E. Shipp

"I sort of like the first day back from vacation ... sort of," Ben said, looking at all the familiar surroundings.

"Yeah ... sort of," Ryan tried to agree. "Well, not really. I had to wake up at seven this morning. That sucked." Ben laughed. He knew how Ryan usually slept in until ten or eleven, sometimes twelve.

They reached their lockers and unloaded everything. Ryan did his usual complaining about the small lockers and how inconvenient they were for all of their classes, and Ben just listened as he usually did. But then, Joe Cossley, who had the locker above Ben's and was probably the tallest guy in school, interrupted Ryan.

Joe was at least six foot five and was, of course, the star basketball player. He had not been held back and did not have growth problems; he was just naturally very tall, just like his parents who were also star sports players. They were divorced, though, so although he was once one of Ben's closest friends in middle school, he was now zoned and cranky all the time, or at least he was when he was around Ben.

"Hey, Joe," Ben said.

"Hmmph," Joe grunted in reply.

Ryan and Ben looked at each other. They finished getting their books out of their lockers and then started walking to the point where they separated for class.

It was on their way to the separating point that they saw them—Jodie *and* Clem walking their way.

"*Whoa!*" Ryan stopped suddenly, staring at the duo as if he had just seen an eclipse of the sun. "*Who* is *that*?"

Ben knew whom he was talking about immediately. He exhaled loudly. "That's Clem. She's our exchange student," he said halfheartedly.

Ryan's jaw dropped to the floor. "*THAT'S* your exchange student? Man ... I hate you!" he said, punching Ben in the arm. "She's *not* living in your house, is she?"

The Lopsided Miracle

"Uh, yeah," Ben said, as if to follow this statement by "duh."

"Ta!" Ryan clucked his tongue on the roof of his mouth. "Dude ..."

"Hey!" Jodie called out to them. Ben noticed color slowly going to Clem's face. Clem smiled at them.

"Hey," Ben said, looking directly at Jodie and not even taking notice of Clem.

Ryan, on the other hand, jumped at the opportunity. "Hi, I'm Ryan." He smiled.

Clem laughed a bit, she was obviously nervous around television stars—or at least guy television stars. "I know, I've seen you ..."

"TV, right?" Ryan said, still staring at her face. Clem bit her lip. Ryan shuddered a little. "Well, I guess I'll see you around then?"

"Yeah." Clem grinned sheepishly. "Definitely."

Jodie looked suspiciously from Clem to Ryan and then simpered. "Well, I guess we will see you around," she said, giving Ryan a few raised eyebrows. Then she walked off to the right, where they had been going in the first place. Clem followed her. Ryan's eyes followed Clem until she turned the corner. He jerked his head back to Ben.

"I'm gonna ask her out," he said, shifting his books to a hip and walking towards the corner where they had just seen Clem and Jodie—the separating point.

"No!" Ben begged. "No, Ryan, please, please don't do that. My life would, like, end."

"What? Man, how could that affect you?"

Ben stared at him as if he had just said pigs could fly. "How could that *affect* me? What kind of a question is that? It's like the whole Marsha deal all over again—but worse, because she lives in my house!" Ben protested.

Ryan just looked at him and then shook his head. "Fine, man. But I *am* going to ask her to the dance in February. The Valentine's Day dance that I always ask Jodie to?"

Emily E. Shipp

"You ask her to go to every dance." Ben laughed.

"Yes, but that was pre-Clem. Now, it's a whole different picture. I mean, come on. Isn't this what you've wanted? If she's my girlfriend, she'll be off your back and so will Jodie. I mean, think about it." The bell rang for classes to begin. Ryan started walking towards his homeroom. "See you," he said.

Ben rolled his eyes and then walked to his homeroom. Mrs. Walsh was there like always. She was a sweet old woman who left her hair down, and it was frizzy like an afro.

He sat in his regular seat right next to Mark, who was, for once, not talking to Marsha. She was in Ryan's homeroom.

"Hiya," Mark said in a fake girly voice. Ben laughed appreciatively. Then, seriously, Mark said, "Do you know who's new in our homeroom?"

Ben shook his head, but before he could say anything, Mrs. Walsh cleared her throat.

"Ladies and gentlemen, quiet down now," Mrs. Walsh said, her voice rough and crackly. "We have a new addition to our homeroom. I hope you will all welcome her in a ... well, I hope you all welcome her warmly." Naturally, the students turned their heads around to see who was new. Ben followed the stares casually. He couldn't really see her because she was in the back row, chatting with a couple of other girls. He turned back around.

"Did you see her?" Mark asked, his tone implying pity. "The rest of the year is going to be bad times for you, bro."

"What?" Ben asked, but just then, Mrs. Walsh addressed the new student to the homeroom.

"I'm Mrs. Walsh, if you didn't know, dear," Mrs. Walsh said to the student. Ben turned around again. Now he could see her since the group blocking his vision had moved, but as soon as he did, he groaned aloud and pounded his head on his desk.

The Lopsided Miracle

It was none other than Fiona Whitewaters, who was waggling her fingers at him in a desperate flirt.

~

"... and then, when you get to be a senior, you, like, get to hang out in this awesome lounge, and I totally can't wait to go! Not to mention that the seniors get all the sweet attention and ..." Katherine Buthe's eyes goggled. "*Who* is *that*?"

She was staring at a new junior who looked as if he had popped out of a Calvin Klein ad. Clem chortled. Katherine Buthe was Jodie's friend, with bright, straight, red hair and skin as pale as milk. She didn't wear braces. Clem decided that Katherine liked to talk ... a little too much.

"He's probably an exchange student," Jodie said, eyeing the figure across the lunchroom who looked like he could pick up a table with his own bare hands.

"Yeah, but where could he be from?" Katherine asked.

While Jodie and Katherine fought over countries that supplied the cutest males, Clem thought over the day so far. It had been a fairly good day. No—it had been a wonderful day. She had been placed in Jodie and Katherine's homeroom and had all her classes with Jodie except for one, drama. But she hoped she would make friends quickly in that class. All her teachers seemed pretty nice and *three* guys (all cute, except for a geek who seemed nice anyway), including *Ryan Matthews*, had started a conversation with her. She smiled at the thought. He was pretty cute, but definitely not Ben, who had seemed reluctant to introduce her to Ryan—the only negative of the day so far.

"What do you think, Clem?" Katherine asked.

Clem snapped out of her thoughts. "What?" She thought quickly. "Um, yeah."

Katherine laughed. "No, which do you think is better guy-wise ... Sweden or Italy?"

Emily E. Shipp

Clem had never been asked a question like that before, so after pondering for about three seconds, she randomly chose a place. "Um ... Italy?"

"Yes! See, Jodie? It's two against one! Majority rules! That guy is from Italy, I'm tellin' ya."

Jodie rolled her eyes. "Right," she said.

Another thing Clem couldn't believe was the name of the school. It was probably the blandest name she had ever come across.

Brown Secondary School.

Not only was the name not fitting for the school because it was made of white brick and glass doors, but it also sounded boring, and the school was anything but. The school was a very active place with weird teachers with wild hairdos and funny voices. The kids were all different with interesting personalities. There were little groups and outcasts, but all in all, they all seemed happy where they were.

"Well, it's off to fifth period," Katherine moaned. "I hate fifth period."

"Really?" Clem asked. "Who do you have?"

"The same person you have, I think. You have Jodie's schedule, right?"

"Yep," Jodie answered for Clem.

"Okay, then you have Mr. Maff. He's a total weirdo. I mean the guy makes us dissect something once a month. Last month's cow heart was not too much fun for anybody."

"Ew," Clem replied, but truthfully she was looking forward to science. It was one of her favorite subjects back at Omega Parsley, but she wasn't about to let that little detail slip to Katherine, who obviously hated it.

The bell rang, and Jodie gathered up all of her trash. Clem copied Jodie's movements, throwing all of it away in the big, black garbage can.

The Lopsided Miracle

"Let's go," Jodie said, laughing at Katherine who was smiling broadly at the Calvin Klein guy.

The drama teacher was a woman who looked about twenty-five and wore cat-eye glasses with little, white, fake diamonds embedded in the purple rim. She wore a multicolored belly dancing skirt and a bright pink marimba shirt with lots of frills and ruffles. She was very tan and wore orange lipstick on her lips, which opened to show teeth as big and straight as a horse's. The first time Clem saw her, she honestly thought that the teacher was a wild and crazy senior.

"Good afternoon, children," the outgoing teacher boomed in the almost empty auditorium. "My name is Ms. Rhododendron, and I ...," she swept her hand in a circle, "... am your drama teacher." A couple of kids looked at each other, and others held back laughter, but Clem just sat in her chair, studying the odd woman. She looked back at Ben, who was sitting a couple of seats beside her. He was looking at Ms. Rhododendron in the same way.

"Drama," she started, "is what most people call acting, some call faking the truth." She grasped her shirt where her heart was, as if this was the most horrible thing that she had ever heard. "I think that everyone should be able to know each other like brothers and sisters when acting, so we are all going to introduce ourselves. Let's start over here." She pointed at Clem. Clem's heart rate leaped up. "You there." Ms. Rhododendron was still pointing. "What is your name?"

Clem stood up shakily and tried to smile at everybody. "I'm, uh, Clem." She looked at Ms. Rhododendron, who was obviously waiting for more. "I, um. I'm from South Carolina, and I'm an exchange student here."

Ms. Rhododendron stared at Clem as if she were an alien. Clem still stood. Ms. Rhododendron shook her head and sighed. "No, no, no. That was all wrong. Get up here." She pointed to the platform in front of herself.

Emily E. Shipp

Clem was caught off guard. "Okay," she murmured. But actually, she had no idea what she had done wrong. She had just mouthed only a couple of words. Like a zombie, she strode up to the small platform in front of the broad, wooden stage.

"Now," Ms. Rhododendron started, crossing her arms across her almost completely flat chest. "Let's try that again. Stand up straight. *Project* your voice. You're not a mouse. You can talk louder than a whisper in *this* class." Some kids near the back rows slapped hands at that statement.

Clem swallowed. "What do you want me to do?" Clem asked, feeling as dumb as an ostrich.

"Pfffh!" Ms. Rhododendron spit. "What do I want you to do? I want you to repeat what you just said, but I want you to project your voice. Everyone, pay attention!" Clem could feel her ears turning as red as tomatoes. She cleared her throat and looked out among the crowd. Everyone was stone-faced and bored, making Clem feel small and helpless. *How can Ben stand to be in front of people like this all the time?* she thought.

She stole a glance at him. For the first time since she had arrived in Canada, he was staring right at her, and his stare wasn't mean. Was it ... encouragement? She cleared her throat again.

"Um, I don't believe that's what you said," Ms. Rhododendron said. The class chuckled. Clem smiled, too, feeling stronger from Ben's glance. She raised her head.

"My name is Clem Greenly, and I'm from South Carolina, and I am an exchange student here at Brown Secondary." Then she decided to be funny, which was definitely unlike quiet and shy Clem. She smiled. "Ma'am, yes, ma'am. That is the truth, the whole truth, and nothing but the truth." The class laughed.

Ms. Rhododendron put on a serious face. All of a sudden, Clem hoped she hadn't said the wrong thing. Ms. Rhododendron walked over

The Lopsided Miracle

to her and glared, but then ended the stare with a laugh. "I like you," she said, patting Clem on the shoulder. "You have spunk."

Clem bit her tongue and went back to her seat. Whatever spunk she had was now gone, she supposed, because Ben wasn't looking at her anymore.

Everyone else in the class, however, was clapping.

CHAPTER ELEVEN

He had not wanted it to happen. He had fought against it more than he fought with Jodie, which, sometimes, was a lot. His conscience and his brain were fighting a war like no other.

It was in drama. The only class where juniors and sophomores mixed, and Clem happened to be in it. When she was called up to do that voice projection, Ben didn't know what happened. It was as if guilt washed over him, and all of a sudden, Clem didn't look like a pest who had taken over his life. She simply looked like a normal sophomore girl, whom everyone crushed on. But this feeing only occurred for a moment. He would have just ignored it, but he feared that Clem had seen him. She had caught his eye when he was feeling that she was sort of ... pretty.

But in his car on the way to the set, he realized that he was just being stupid. Just because the lighting was weird didn't mean that all of a sudden he had to forgive her for what she had done to his life.

He shook his head as he pulled into the set, saying hi to the police guard on the way in.

"Did anyone actually memorize their lines for today?" Mark asked, sitting in the back of Ben's car.

Ryan laughed. "No one ever does. But hey, that's why they have bloopers, right?" Ryan said.

Ben nodded and then remembered something. "Hey, are we all still on for tomorrow night's band practice?" Ben asked.

Mark gasped and then hit his head. "Aw crap! I forgot!" he growled under his breath.

Ben rolled his eyes. "What?" he asked, parking in the small lot by the set.

"I made a date with Marsha. I forgot all about it."

Emily E. Shipp

Ben opened his door, hopped out, and slammed the door shut again. He had been in a good mood, but now it was shattered. Mark was really getting on his nerves. Why was he ditching band practice? There were only three of them to begin with anyway, not enough to hold a practice without him.

Why was his life getting more and more complicated?

Then, when he was walking into the makeup area, he spotted another car coming up the lot. It was Mrs. Clavis's car, dropping off Jodie. But someone else was with her, and Ben knew who it was—Clem. He groaned and kept walking to the makeup trailer. He wasn't going to let Clem ruin his time at the set, no matter what happened. This was one thing she couldn't touch, no matter how hard she tried.

~

Clem got out of the car and looked around. It was absolutely a dream come true. Such pride filled her when she put her foot down on the pavement. It was like her first period. She felt older, wiser somehow. This was something she would tell her grandchildren when she was eighty years old. *Yes, I was on the set of my favorite TV show when I was your age.*

"Well, here it is. Home sweet set," Jodie said. Clem giggled. "Let me show you around."

"This is great," Clem said, following Jodie to the makeup trailer.

"I guess," Jodie said. "You kind of get used to it. I mean it's not that glamorous once you think about it. It's just normal people being recorded on tape." Clem raised her eyebrow. Jodie laughed. "Okay, never mind. It's more than that."

Jodie pushed open the door. Clem saw Ben, Mark, and Ryan already sitting down to get their makeup done. Jodie said hello to all of them, and they all replied with friendly hellos.

Then Ryan smiled at Clem. "Hey, Clem," he said.

The Lopsided Miracle

Clem bared her teeth in a friendly manner. "Hey, Ryan," she said, tossing her hair over her shoulder. She was still in her clothes from school. In fact, everyone was, except for the makeup artists of course.

Jodie sat down in a chair next to Ben and a woman with dark curls came out of a tiny hallway. She greeted Jodie.

"Hey, babe! How was your vacation?" she asked, showing off a toothy smile.

"It was good!" Jodie said. The woman immediately got to work doing Jodie's hair and makeup, even though she already had some makeup on.

"Clem, this is Victoria, my makeup artist. She works magic," Jodie teased.

"Oh, stop it," Victoria said. She looked about thirty or so. While Victoria applied curlers to Jodie's hair, she took a peek at Clem. "You don't look so bad yourself," Victoria complimented Clem.

Clem grinned, but in her mind, thoughts were racing. *What is with these people? Do I really look that great? Why is everyone complimenting me?* She looked at herself in the mirror. She looked just like her old self.

"Thank you, ma'am," Clem said. She watched everyone as they were getting their makeup done. She couldn't help but envy them. Oh, how she wished she could be in one of those chairs! The odd thing was, though, that none of them were bragging or acting like celebrities. Clem didn't understand.

Once Jodie was done and Victoria had said, "You look darling, babe," they left for Jodie's trailer.

"Wow, you get your own trailer?" Clem asked in amusement.

Jodie grinned. "Yeah, it's okay," she said. They walked up the narrow steps and into the rickety, silver door.

Clem looked around inside. It was a normal trailer (well, Clem supposed it was normal—she had never seen one before, except in the makeup area), but to Clem, it seemed like a castle. It was what every

Emily E. Shipp

teenage girl would want to show off—because it meant you had an interesting, famous life. It had a comfy, green couch and a refrigerator filled with Cokes and other various brands of pop. The trailer had cabinets filled with paper plates and cups, and drawers with plastic knives and spoons. The empty walls were covered with pictures from magazines. It was perfect.

"This is awesome," Clem commented.

"Thanks," Jodie said. "It's where I usually spend my breaks. Either here or playing cards over by the set. Do you want to see the set?"

Clem's heart fluttered. *Did she want to see the set?* "Um, duh." Clem smiled excitedly. Scarlett was going to flip out!

"Okay," Jodie said, opening the door again, "you might want to keep a close follow. It's pretty big."

Clem laughed a little too loudly. "Oh, I'll know my way around, I think. I mean, I watch your show every day!" Then it occurred to her that she hadn't seen any episodes since she had arrived in Toronto. She shook the thought aside. After all, she would have been embarrassed out of her wits if any of the Clavises had seen her watching the show. Actually, now that she thought about it, she was frustrated at herself for telling Jodie her little secret. She didn't know why; she just felt a little immature being the only girl on the set who was a fan and not actually on the job.

"Really?" Jodie didn't look surprised. "I wouldn't have guessed." Clem really regretted her words when she looked at Jodie's face and saw that she was lying. "Well, here's the 'school,'" Jodie said, opening a door.

Clem looked inside this huge set. It looked a lot different than what she had expected. It didn't look like a school at all. Just a couple of hallways here and there, and classrooms scattered all over. It was odd to see it in such a state. On television, it really looked like a school.

"It … looks different," Clem said.

The Lopsided Miracle

Jodie giggled. "I know. It looks a lot different on TV, doesn't it?" She was reading Clem's mind.

Clem nodded. "Yeah."

"Jodie! There you are!" The two girls whipped around. A man with a bright yellow tuxedo was coming out of a small office in the corner of a huge room that Clem had somehow missed. Jodie sighed.

"Hey, Joe." Jodie turned to Clem. "That is Joe Carton. He's sort of ..."

Clem looked at his ensemble. "Off?" Clem suggested.

"No, no," Jodie said, as he came closer, "just a little ... strange ... sometimes."

"Jodie! Hello! I'm so glad I found you! We have a few special guests in my office. Do you mind?" He looked over Jodie's head as if expecting to see a criminal jump out from behind a camera. Clem noticed that this "Joe" seemed very flustered, like he was fighting with something but being rational at the same time. This was the same "something" Clem had found to be very exhausting during her debate with her mother about the whole exchange student thing. Clem smiled at Joe without showing any teeth. He saw her and then looked at Jodie.

"Jodie? Where is your brother? And how many times do I have to tell you not to bring any of your friends to the set?"

"This is our exchange student, Clem," Jodie said. "I thought I would show her around."

"Oh, really?" Joe Carton seemed to brighten at this news. He smiled at Clem, as if she were a dog about to run away when he had been trying to catch her for an hour. "Clem is your name? Very exotic, may I say."

What is he doing? Clem thought immediately. *Why is he coaxing me like that?* She raised an eyebrow. "Um, thank you," she said.

Jodie looked suspicious, too. "Joe, can I say that you're acting very ..."

Emily E. Shipp

"Clem, have you ever been on television? In a movie? In the ... newspaper, perhaps?" He asked, letting go of Jodie and putting his arm around Clem. He reminded Clem a little of Hitler. Clem shook his hand off, but couldn't help wondering what he meant.

"No," Clem said, "not that I can remember."

"Well." Joe's face stretched into a broad smile. "How would you like to be in the news ... right now?"

~

"I hear from Mrs. Bertha Queenly that you have taken in an exchange student. Is this true?" asked a woman with a short, beige skirt, full hair, and red, pouty lips. Ben blinked. He had been asked these ridiculous questions ever since he got out of makeup. He was going to have nightmares for a week about Mrs. Queenly saying the same thing: *What could be more news-friendly than having two young actors take in a random fan and treat them to their humble homes and lives? How ingenious!*

"What is living with a complete stranger like?" The woman asked another question.

... Treat them to their humble homes and lives?

"Is this affecting your school life any more than it has already been affected by the television show?"

...Homes and lives...

"Excuse me ..."

... Lives ...

"Excuse me? Ben?" Ben shook his head, clearing away the horrible ringing voice, echoing through his brain. He sighed, and with a body that seemed as though it were full of lead, he answered questions until Joe Carton came walking through the door, dragging Clem along behind him. Jodie was there, too, looking as confused as Clem, until she saw the news reporters leaning against the walls, waiting for their turns to get information for their own newspapers. Ben took one glance at his

The Lopsided Miracle

sister's face and knew that she remembered Mrs. Queenly's words at that moment, too. She gulped. Clem still looked a little befuddled.

Mrs. Queenly's face turned from satisfied to thankful. She walked over to Clem. "Joe, is this ..."

"This is the exchange student," he said. "Things are going very well, don't you think?"

Mrs. Queenly nodded. Then she turned to the huddles of reporters. "Everyone, I think you'll be very pleased to know that along with interviewing these two ..." she gestured toward the two star siblings, "...you will also be able to interview another. The exchange student herself," she trumpeted. All of a sudden, the reporters started bustling around, making even more noise than they had before.

Ben turned around to see Joe Carton and Mrs. Queenly allow the reporters with their notepads and pens flailing, grab at Clem's arms and shove her into a chair. Jodie and Ben were already suffocating in the hot, stuffy room, and now that the reporters were active, it was even worse.

"Ben," Jodie said. He turned toward her while the blond-haired reporter started writing things down. "Are you okay with this?"

Ben nodded shakily. "I guess so. We've done this before, right?" he said.

Jodie furrowed her eyebrows. "Well, yeah, but look at Clem," she said.

Ben did. Why was Jodie concerned? Clem looked flattered. He shrugged. "She'll deal with it," he said. Jodie turned back around, looking a little more at ease. "Okay, I don't know why you're worried. She's in the news, right? She should be thanking us," Ben said.

Jodie nodded. "I guess," she said, staring at a balding man who was coming towards her. "Yeah. I mean, she's never been in the news before; this is something cool for her. I don't know what I'm so worried about."

Emily E. Shipp

But Ben had a feeling that she *did* have something to be worried about; Ben just didn't know what.

CHAPTER TWELVE

It had been a very weird day—very weird indeed. Clem had been confronted by all these different reporters asking her different questions like, "How is it—living with two television stars?" and "Did you know what you might get yourself into when you entered your name in the exchange program?" and "Have you ever seen the show before?" Clem wanted to laugh at that question. Had she ever seen the show before? Of course! She answered all the reporters' questions. She had never been interviewed before, and she found it exhilarating.

She could see Jodie's worried glance, looking over her shoulder at Clem. Clem didn't understand why she was giving her those looks, but her thoughts were interrupted by a tall, uptight-looking woman with black hair tied in a bun. She started talking to the man in the yellow suit, Joe.

"I told you this would work out," she bragged. "All these reporters ... it's wonderful."

"Yes, it was a brilliant idea," Joe Carton said a little dully. The woman didn't seem to notice. Clem felt a little like she was in an old western movie overhearing the bandits. She was getting bad vibes from this woman.

"I knew this would pay off. Anyway, *I'm* going to get paid for such a good story. Even if I do have to pay those little brats double the amount they were making, I'm going to be able to get it back so easily. I'm telling you, the way you have to bribe kids these days." Clem widened her eyes at this news, but had no time to reflect on it, because a news reporter sat in the seat across from her.

"Hello, I'm John O'Neil, News Four," he introduced himself. Clem couldn't honestly care less about what the reporter was saying after what she had just overheard from the woman. *Little brats? Paid double?*

Emily E. Shipp

They were getting paid double? Why? Is it because of ... me? Clem thought. She wondered if this was why Jodie had looked over at her in such a fashion—because Clem might find out why she was there in the first place. Well, now she knew. They hadn't wanted her there. They were only hosting her because they were getting paid double. Clem's whole body shook. Did that mean Jodie had lied about wanting to be friends? It hadn't seemed that way, but then again, Jodie seemed pretty sneaky now.

She had only known Jodie for a couple of days, but what betrayal!

She answered the rest of the reporters' questions stone-faced. She didn't care if she was from America or that she had only known Jodie for less than a week. She was mad. She had been so excited about their wanting her to be there, but they hadn't. Not at all.

It seemed like forever before every last reporter left the premises. Clem's expression hadn't changed a bit. As soon as the reporter questioning Jodie left, Jodie leaped up and ran over to Clem, who was now standing.

"Oh my gosh, Clem, I am *SO* sorry. I didn't know it was going to be like that. I thought it was just going to be a normal day here."

"Why didn't you tell me?" Clem asked.

Jodie's eyebrows made crinkles on the bridge of her nose. "What?" she said croakily. All that talking was hard on the throat.

Clem almost backed out right there, seeing that she was new and all. But this was serious. "I mean, not that it's my business or anything, but why didn't you tell me that you didn't want me here? Maybe I should just leave, that would be another story for you to make money on." *Okay*, Clem's conscience started roaring, *that was a little harsh*. But Clem couldn't stop,

"What? Clem ...—"

"Oh, no. I forgot. I *can't* leave. If I did, then you wouldn't be able to get paid double!" she said loudly. "Am I right?" she ended quietly.

The Lopsided Miracle

Jodie was gawking at Clem like she was an alien from Mars. All of a sudden, her chest heaved up and down and she closed her eyes. "*This* is what I was afraid of," she said, her voice sounding as small as a mouse's.

"So ... it's the truth then? You don't want me here!" Clem said intently.

"No," Jodie interrupted, her hand cutting in front of Clem like a police officer stopping someone from crossing the street. "That's not true."

"Really? Then why ...—"

"Would you please listen to me?" Jodie asked fiercely. Clem shrunk back. She had had all the power up until then. *Why don't I ever listen to myself?* she thought. Jodie was very serious, and even though Clem felt as though her anger level was a ten out of ten, Jodie deserved to be listened to, even if it was for an excuse.

"Look, when it first started out," Jodie began, "Mrs. Queenly, the woman with the black hair? Yeah, well, she told us that we were losing publicity and we had to do something about it." She sighed. "So she thought we could enter an exchange student program and take in a fan or something. Neither Ben nor I liked the idea at first, but then she said that she would pay us double what we get for our normal wages here, so we accepted. We didn't have the slightest idea it was going to be you then.

"When you came here, I was so psyched because you were a girl exactly my age and all that. I was so happy for you to be here, and I really did want you to be my friend. It was just today that I remembered Mrs. Queenly and ... I was worried that this would happen." Clem just stood there, thinking everything over. Jodie laughed. "But listen to me. I sound as sappy as a tree." She smiled. "I'm really sorry, Clem."

Clem agreed about the sappy part. She was so very relieved after all of this and wanted to kick herself in the head for being so ...

Emily E. Shipp

jumping-to-conclusions-ish. Now she really felt as though she was in a movie, and she knew what was next on the script.

"Okay," Clem said, half-smiling. "That's a relief." Still feeling tension in the air, she cracked another comment. "Did I ever tell you you're a very good public speaker? That speech you just gave was about as good as a teacher's."

Now Jodie really laughed. "Is that a good thing?" she asked, laughing still. "Besides, if I was a bad public speaker, would I even be here in the first place?"

Clem shrugged. "I guess not," she said. They started walking. "Another thing," Clem said as Jodie led her out the door and to the open parking lot. "Did you know that Mrs. Queery— "

"Queenly," Jodie corrected.

"Whatever." Clem brushed her mistake off like a fly in the summer. "Did you know that she calls you guys little brats?"

Jodie chuckled, remembering the shrimp cocktail incident. "Actually ... I'm not really very surprised," she said.

~

"Can't buy me loooooooove, oh! Loooooooove, oh! Can't buy me loooooooove, oh! Oh!" Ryan was rocking his little heart out in the booth at the Pizza Plaza where he and Ben had decided to eat after the confusing day. The music, which was coming out of the jukebox in the old-style restaurant, was a Beatles song, and Ryan was getting into it like he did in his garage with the band. "... Buy me diamond rings, my friend, if it makes you feel alright ..."

"Excuse me, Ringo, do you know what you want?" Ben interrupted.

Ryan laughed. "No, no. I'm John Lennon. Can't you tell?" He struck a pose.

Ben stared blankly. "Do you want me to answer that?" he asked. Out of the corner of his eye, he saw a waitress coming towards

The Lopsided Miracle

them. She was short and busty and was wearing the black-and-white checkered uniform that all the waitresses were required to wear. She looked about seventeen.

"Hey, hun!" The waitress said as if she knew them. Ben almost laughed aloud. Of course she knew them. They were on billboards for goodness sake. "Aren't you on TV or somethin'?" She snapped her gum.

"Yeah," Ben said. He stole a look at Ryan, who was still playing an invisible drum set. The girl laughed. Ben grinned.

"Who's your friend?" she asked Ben flirtatiously. His smile vanished. She was nice enough, but then she seemed to like Ryan instead. Being famous didn't have advantages *all* the time. He sighed, not answering.

"Can we please have combo number four with extra fries?" he asked. The girl gave him a sour look when he didn't answer her question, but she reluctantly wrote the order down on her little pink pad and stomped off. Ben continued to watch Ryan.

"Ryan?" he asked after a while. Ryan was still bobbing his head to the music. Once the music was over, he opened his eyes, which had been closed as he imagined himself in front of an adoring crowd. Then he took a long, sickening gulp of Mango Yellow and gave a satisfied sigh.

"Ryan?" Ben asked again.

"Yeah," Ryan said distractedly.

"You're a dork. Didn't you just see that?" He waved his hand carelessly toward the waitress who was now taking someone else's order.

"See what?" Ryan asked, clueless.

Ben banged his hand on his head. "That waitress! She was, like, totally checkin' you out!" Ben said.

It took Ryan a little while to figure this out. Then he smiled and shook his finger at Ben. "Ah, yes, grasshopper. But, have you already forgotten?" he asked.

Ben decided that Ryan was definitely losing brain cells by rocking his head with the drums. No one with the right amount of brain cells would call him "grasshopper." "Frankly, right now I don't remember much," Ben said truthfully.

"Clem," Ryan said.

Ben closed his eyes. It was on the tip of his tongue to tell Ryan that he was being crazy—why would he want to go out with Clem? But something was holding him back. Something he couldn't identify. He shook his head vigorously. What was he thinking? This was the second time today! He was going absolutely crazy thinking Clem was anything but a menace!

"Whatever," Ben said, taking a drink of his Coke.

"Here ya go, babe." The waitress was back. Ben could tell that she was a lot more interested in trying to get Ryan's attention, seeing that she was putting the whole pizza platter on his side. She put the two orders of fries there, too. Ryan grinned his "you're too kind" grin at her. She almost fainted and breathed in a big gulp of air, but managed to stagger off.

Ben laughed. "Player," he said, taking a piece of pizza and shoving it into his mouth.

Ryan shrugged. "No, I was just being polite, couldn't you tell?" Ryan asked.

Ben raised an eyebrow. "Do you truthfully want me to answer that?"

~

Clem woke up the next morning feeling sort of grungy. She felt old and tired, like she hadn't slept for weeks. She didn't quite know why she felt this way; she thought she should have felt good since

The Lopsided Miracle

she had cleared things up with Jodie, but all in all, she felt bad. She decided to take a shower, thinking that maybe it would clear some of her thoughts.

She got out of bed and staggered over to the bathroom. She would have swung open the door as she had done the day before, but she was not about to make the same mistake twice. She knocked twice, lightly with her knuckles. Maybe Ben was in there and hadn't heard her? Oh well, she thought. It wasn't as if she minded seeing him half-nude.

She opened the door, but to her slight disappointment, he was nowhere to be seen. Clem shrugged, closed the door, locked it, and did the same with the door leading from the hallway. She opened the shower curtain and looked at the faucet. She had just learned how to use it a couple of days ago. She started it, took off her pajamas, and stepped in. It was a little hot at first, but it woke her up immediately.

In the middle of shaving her legs, she heard a knock on the door. It startled her so much that she almost nicked herself. At that moment, she realized that she had walked in on Ben when he was shaving—not his legs, but his face. She smiled. What a coincidence. She put her razor down and poked her head out from behind the curtain.

"Who is it?" she called out.

"Ben," she heard him mumble. Her mouth dropped open. She started to panic. What was she going to do? Then she thought that she was being way too paranoid, which she was.

"Um, can you hold on a sec?" Clem called.

Ben grunted, as he usually did when talking to Clem. But then, to her surprise, he said, "Yeah, sure."

Clem had never had the time to find out why he disliked her so, but that didn't mean that the question had completely dropped out of her mind. She still really wanted to know, since to her, Ben was the world.

She finished quickly, jumped out, and dried herself frantically. She combed her hair, wrapped a towel around her torso, and then

Emily E. Shipp

opened the door to go back into her room but rushed right back in when she saw Ben standing right on the other side of the door.

"Ah!" she screamed. She had never heard herself scream in such a high-pitched manner before, but there it was—that loud scream.

She heard Ben sigh and then say, "You know, Clem. This is really going to be a problem."

"Well, words," Katherine observed. "That's coming along."

Clem shook her head. "I don't like him, okay?" Clem said. Even though she was telling a huge lie when she said this, she said it anyway.

Katherine laughed. "Yeah right. You just happen to bring up how Ben actually said something to you this morning in the middle of us talking about Mr. Italy over there." She raised her eyebrows at the buff exchange student that she had been ogling over yesterday. Just as she was talking about him, he turned around to them, smiled, and got up out of his chair. Katherine grabbed Jodie's arm.

"Oh, my God!" Katherine screeched. "Oh ... omigod. He's coming over here," she observed. She immediately started straightening her hair, picking food out of her teeth, and brushing her bangs out of her eyes. She smiled sweetly at the boy as he walked over. Unfortunately for Katherine, he didn't walk over to her; he walked straight to Clem.

"Hi," he said in a voice that sounded deep and soothing. It also sounded Swedish.

"Hey." Clem smiled. While Jodie was panting slightly and Katherine's eyes were almost popping out of her head, Clem couldn't help but think how Ben Clavis looked better to her.

"I'm Joel Marion. I'm an exchange student from Zweden." Katherine giggled. Joel kept on talking, "Aren't you from America?"

"Yes, she is," Katherine intruded, shoving Clem over to one side while she took the spotlight, "but I'm from ...," she swished her hair

The Lopsided Miracle

dramatically, "... Canada." She blinked her eyes several times while Joel stared at her with a questioning look on his face.

"I zaw you in za paper," he went on, talking to Clem.

Jodie all of a sudden took action. She grabbed the paper from Joel without even asking for it and stared at the black-and-white words. Then she smiled, handing it over to Clem. "Hey," she said, "you're in the paper!" Clem looked down at it. There was a picture of her sitting in a chair in that small corner office at the set. She didn't want to toot her own horn, but she didn't look all that bad.

"Wow," Katherine said. "I've known Jodie for all my life, and *I've* never been in the paper!" she complained, but she smiled and looked at the picture, too. "I am so jealous!"

Clem knew that she was going to have to cut out the article to send to Scarlett as soon as she could.

"Hey, Joel," Clem asked. Joel looked up. "Could I borrow this?"

Joel nodded. "Of courze," he said in a strong Swedish accent.

Clem smiled. "Thanks," Clem said.

"Yeah, thankz ...uh, I mean ..." Katherine blushed. "Thanks."

Joel laughed a very manly laugh. "No problem." He grinned. "What iz your name?"

"Oh, um, Katherine ... Joel." She beamed. Joel nodded his head, waved, and walked back to his table, which was filled with players on the football team.

"Yeah ... bye," Katherine said quietly, still staring at him. Jodie burst out with a wave of giggling that rang across the cafeteria. Clem couldn't help but chuckle, too.

Katherine glared at them. "What?" she snapped.

Jodie just gave her answer with a laugh.

~

"Why are we friends?" Ryan asked at break.

Ben was caught off guard at this question, but answered anyway. "I don't know. Is this a trick question?" he asked.

"No," Ryan said, whipping out the newspaper. Ben rolled his eyes. Ryan was now carrying around that paper as if it were the Bible. "But this is a very tricky situation."

"What are you talking about?"

"You know what I mean," Ryan said. "God. I mean this girl is like ... a *model*. I mean, I even saw that Joel character hanging on her at lunch."

"Let him," Ben said. But for some reason, he felt a pang of jealousy.

"What?" Ryan said. "Man, I don't think I will ever get you at all."

"Hey!" Mark snuck up on them. For once, he wasn't with Marsha.

"Where's the GF?" Ben asked.

"Nah, I dumped her," Mark said. "I was just talking to Fiona, and Marsha totally went ballistic. But anyway, speaking of Fiona, she was wondering if she could sit with you at lunch." He pretended to curl his hair around his finger girlishly. "Oh, please. He's just *dashing*." Ryan cracked up.

"Not funny. And why were you talking to Fiona anyway?" Ben asked, smiling at a girl walking by in the hall. The girl gasped and started chatting to her friends. Ben couldn't help but notice that there was another girl among them that he knew—Fiona Whitewaters. Fiona craned her neck to see him walk by with his backpack slung carelessly over one shoulder.

"Oh great, hide," Ben said, but it was too late. Fiona started shuffling over to where the trio was standing.

"Hi, Ben!" she squealed.

Ben looked over to his friends who were now trying desperately not to laugh. "Um, hi, Fiona," Ben said. "I have to get to ...—"

The Lopsided Miracle

"That's great. You'll never guess what Ms. Rhodie said. She thinks we'll be doing *Cinderella* for the school play this year. Isn't that just *fab*?" she asked.

No, it is not fab, Ben wanted to say, but held himself back. Ms. Rhododendron, or Ms. Rhodie as she was more commonly called, was a very cool, um ... different person, but at that moment, Ben didn't want to talk about her.

"I have to get to class, Fiona," he explained, pulling himself away from her.

She let out a disappointed sigh. "Oh, Ben. Don't be ridiculous. Class doesn't start for another ...," she checked her baby blue watch, "...four minutes," she declared. She grabbed the crook of his arm and started pulling him toward her gang of friends who were all giggling like chirping birds.

"I think we'll leave you two *alone*," Mark said. Ryan was already walking away laughing ferociously. Ben gave him a glare that said, *We're not finished ...*

"Oh, they're so funny," Fiona chuckled.

Ben smirked. "Yeah, real funny," he said, as he was being forced toward the circle of girls.

The one whom he had smiled at walked over to him. "Hi, Ben," she said, handing Fiona the paper.

Fiona grabbed it and scowled at her drones. "Ex-*cuse* me, a little privacy?" she said as if they were supposed to know firsthand to leave. Everyone's smiles were dimmed, but they left at their leader's command.

"Ah-hem, okay. That's much better," she said when they were a ways down the hall. "Now." She jerked the paper upright from its crooked position. She forced a laugh and then pointed to the picture of Clem. Her smile faded.

Emily E. Shipp

"I recognized that girl, you know. She's in our drama class. That … sophomore …" She wrinkled her nose, acting like Clem had cooties. "It's not true, is it?"

For a moment, Ben felt a pang of worry. "Um, what?" he asked.

She let out an exasperated breath. "You know what I mean," she said.

Ben furrowed his eyebrows. "Why is everyone saying that today?" he asked. In fact, he hadn't read the article, but was all of a sudden wanting to. "Can I please borrow that paper?" he asked.

Fiona made her eyes into little slits. "So it *is* true?" she asked.

"No," Ben tried to explain, "I don't even know what's going on."

Fiona then smiled again, showing off all her teeth and a lot of her gums. But it was a very mischievous smile. "Oh, well, I think you'll … um … *enjoy* reading this." She thrust the paper in his chest, and Ben caught it in his arms. She walked away, moving her hips from side to side in a trying-to-be-casual-but-actually-looking-like-a-hippo manner.

Ben stifled a laugh, and as he was about to read the column, he overheard Fiona talking to one of her followers who had chosen to stay behind. "No worries, Abby," she said. Ben realized that it was the girl who had handed Fiona the paper—the same girl he had smiled at. He had never really seen her before, but he guessed she was Fiona's best friend out of her gang of drones.

"Really? So it's a lie?" Abby asked.

Fiona smirked, and they started hip waggling away. "I suppose, but anyway, this means that I have a date for the Valentine's Day dance.—"

Ben couldn't hear the rest, but wanted to know immediately what she was talking about. He looked down at the paper, wide-eyed and anxious. But after a few moments, he dropped the paper on the floor and ran towards the boy's bathroom, feeling extremely sick.

Right under Clem's picture was the caption, "Clementine Greenly, exchange student and girlfriend of Benjamin Clavis."

CHAPTER THIRTEEN

"AHHHHH!!" Clem screamed. It was that same high-pitched scream she had screamed when she had walked out of the bathroom and met Ben. The only difference was that this was longer than a short squeal. It was a long, high scream.

Jodie burst through the door of the girls' bathroom, carrying another copy of the newspaper. Her hair was falling out of the perfect ponytail it had been set up in just that morning. She was *that* frazzled.

"Clem? You're in here, right?" Jodie started banging open every stall, finding all except one empty (that one was locked, of course) until she reached Clem's, which was on the very end.

"Jodie." Clem started breathing very fast. "Omigod, omigod ..."

"Wait," Jodie said. She craned her neck to look out from the stall. The girl who had been in the stall was now washing her hands very slowly. She was obviously an eavesdropper.

"Get out of here! Can't you see we have a crisis?" she yelled at the girl. The girl jumped, obviously startled, and without even drying her hands off, she rushed out of the bathroom. Jodie rolled her eyes and turned back to Clem.

"Jodie ... oh ..." Clem covered her face. "This is horrible. You're seeing me, like, completely freaking out ..."

"It's no problem," Jodie said, pointing to the paper, "but this may be one." Clem closed her eyes, still panting. Was this a panic attack?

"I read everything. I can't believe it's sixth period, and I've *just* heard about it! And *I'm* the host of the exchange student they lied about!" She gave Clem a weird look. "It *is* a lie, isn't it?"

"Yes!" Clem wailed, secretly wishing it wasn't.

Emily E. Shipp

"Okay, okay," Jodie said. Clem noticed that her cheeks were flushed, too. "Ugh! I am so mad at those reporters! They made you look so shallow!"

Clem raised an eyebrow.

"Well." Jodie shrugged. "What can I say? My bro *is* shallow. So they're making readers think that you're shallow enough to go out with him."

"Gee," Clem said. "Thanks."

"Well, you know what I mean. But is that what's wrong?" Jodie asked.

"No," Clem replied, "it's not that. It's just ... I'm so humiliated! What if Ben thinks I actually lied and said that I was his girlfriend just so that I could make people think it? I'm sure that's what he thinks! This is awful ..." Clem moaned.

Jodie patted her shoulder. "Don't worry about that. I'm in the TV industry, remember? I'll have this straightened up as soon as I can."

It was true. Clem was comforted some by those words, but what would Ben think in the meantime? She hadn't talked to him yet and wasn't really sure she would have the courage to now. "I know, but I have drama with Ben. I won't even be able to look at him without feeling embarrassed."

"Well then, don't look at him. It's not like you do ... anyway ...?" All of a sudden, Jodie got a weird look in her eye again.

Clem was quick to deny. "No! Never. I don't like him. I don't even look at him at all. Never, no." But she knew she sounded stupid.

The corners of Jodie's mouth started to turn upward. "You *do* like him ..."

"No!" Clem was never going to tell the truth about that. Not to Jodie, and especially not to Ben. "Listen. You told me to always remember you as just Jodie. Remember that?" Jodie nodded, still with a curved lip. "But now you have to trust me. You *cannot* think of me as

The Lopsided Miracle

just a love-struck fan. I don't like Ben. Okay?" She was so demanding she surprised herself.

She guessed that she surprised Jodie too because her smile was gone and she was lifting her shoulders instead. "Okay," she said. "You actually had me worried there for a second."

You had me worried, too, Clem thought.

"Well, it's off to seventh," Jodie said, heading out of the stall and throwing both copies of the newspaper in the garbage can under the paper towel dispenser.

"Don't remind me," Clem grumbled.

Jodie laughed a bit. "Hey, stop worrying! Everything will be okay. I've got a new episode we're shooting today. We were supposed to practice yesterday, but you know how things worked out."

Yes, I do, Clem thought miserably.

"Anyway, I'll fix things today with Joe. Remember? The guy wearing the yellow?"

Clem nodded, remembering with only half of her thoughts. The other half was fretting. *You've only been here two days and already you're way too popular!* Clem's conscience told her. Clem agreed.

This was the worst start ever!

~

"Now, I know we've just gotten back from our Christmas breaks and everyone's still trying to get in the groove of things," Ms. Rhodie said, doing a funky hand motion, "but we've got to start on our play so that we can do it by the deadline I set. Sound good to everyone?"

"When are we casting characters?" Fiona piped. Ben slunk down in his seat. He didn't want to be seen by Clem, Ms. Rhodie, or anybody else. It was horrible sitting all alone, but Joe Cossley was absent, and Ben usually sat with him in drama. Also, everyone was giving him strange looks; it seemed like the whole school had read the newspaper.

Emily E. Shipp

He was so mad at Clem. He had started to think he was being paranoid about Clem ruining his life, but now she really *had!*

"Hold on, Miss Whitewaters. I haven't even told the class what play I've decided on yet." Fiona gave Ben a look. He avoided it. He was too busy trying to burn a hole through Clem's skull.

"Well, everyone." Ms. Rhodie clapped her hands together. "We're going to do the classic *Cinderella*!"

There were a lot of grunts and groans from the guys and a lot of excited squeals from the girls, including Fiona, Abby, and two other girls from their clique.

"Now, now," Ms. Rhodie said, addressing the boys, "this will be fun!" Following the groans, there were eye-rolls. Ms. Rhodie chose to ignore these motions. "Now, since I don't know who's going to be playing whom, I've decided to just give out random parts to random people—well, you aren't all random, but you know what I mean," Ms. Rhodie said. "So if you'll all come up to the stage ..."

Everyone lazily got out of their auditorium seats and slumped up the stage steps. The auditorium was probably one of Ben's favorite places—it was just a massive amount of nothing but empty chairs waiting to be filled and a stage on which he was to act. When he had first joined the drama club, he had considered it something different to try out, but then, once he got the leading role on *The Truth Told by Me*, he began to love acting. And the staff didn't exactly dislike the amount of people he drew to their plays. Most of them only came to the plays because he was famous.

But now he sat on the stage, cross-legged and slouched, and grabbed a copy of the play that Ms. Rhodie was handing out. Fiona plopped down right next to him, bringing several other girls with her. He took a peek at the size of the script and sighed when he saw that it was very thick. He didn't know how much he would have to memorize for the show, but since the cast of his show knew about Ben's school plays, they always tried to make equal time for the show and the play. The only

The Lopsided Miracle

reason they did this, though, was because so many people came to the performance, which gained good publicity. This idea was, of course, Mrs. Queenly's.

"Okay, everyone," Ms. Rhodie started talking again. Ben flipped from the cover page to the first act. Ms. Rhodie started giving out parts carelessly. "... Abby, you can be the king for now. No, no, you won't be a boy for the real thing. Fiona? Yes, Fiona, stop talking and pay attention. You can be the queen ..." Ben started to zone everything out except for Clem who was sitting cross-legged too, looking perfectly normal. Ben knew she was really satisfied with her evil, evil plan to destroy him ...

"Ben? Ben, are you listening?" Ben zapped back into reality and shook his head to relieve some thoughts. He nodded and cleared his throat. "Yeah, I'm here." Fiona laughed loudly at his comment, even though it was not meant to jest, and Clem gave a small smile.

"Well, all right then. You can be the evil stepmother for right now." The whole class laughed now, but Ben noticed Clem was stiff and was only expressing slight chuckles. If she was so satisfied, then wouldn't she be a little more comfortable?

She knows that she's in over her head, Ben decided. *She'll be sorry she ever said that to those reporters ...*

"Okay." Ben nodded his head, as if comprehending that he was going to act out the evil stepmother. "I can deal with that."

"Good," Ms. Rhodie said. "Now ..." She kept giving off roles until she reached Clem. "Ah." She smiled. "We've reached the outgoing one!" She said it in a good way, but Clem still blushed. Ben disgustedly remembered when she had made a good impression on most of the kids in the drama class as she had introduced herself. "Why don't we cast you as Cinderella herself for now? Let's give you a shot."

Ben almost laughed aloud for two reasons. If she even thought she had a chance at being Cinderella, then she was going to have a tough time. Fiona Whitewaters always got what she wanted in these things, so there was a nearly invisible chance for Clem to get that role.

Emily E. Shipp

Secondly, the situation was too perfect: Clem as Cinderella and Ben as the evil stepmother? This was going to be excellent...

"Okay!" said Ms. Rhodie. "Begin ..."

Ben was zoning again, but this time, he wasn't zoning out—he was zoning in. He was focusing so much on his first lines that his eyeballs almost exploded from the sockets. Only two more pages to go ... one page ... *flip, flip* ... He was almost there...

"Oh, stepmother," Clem recited in her Cinderella voice, "why are you so mean to me? Whatever have I done?" Ben looked at Clem. Clem shifted her gaze from the words to meet Ben's gaze.

He gave her a sly grin. "What have you done?" Ben said, reading from the script and acting out in an old, witchy sort of tone. Some people giggled at his fake girl voice. "*What have you done*? What a ridiculous question. You, *you* are the one who made your father die! You are the one who has left me with all of this to bear. Do you understand how *hard* this is for me, *Cinder*ella?" Ben acted. His lines were over, but he had more to say.

He wasn't afraid. He wanted to speak, so he was going to speak. Cutting the next character off, he continued—not in a fake voice anymore. "Yes," he said. "Do you know how hard this is for me? Do you know how so incredibly awful it is for me to have you here? Eating my food? Sharing my house? You make me absolutely sick. I hate your guts. I hate the cytoplasm in the *cells* of your guts. I hate everything about you. You ruined everything for me. I wish you would just leave." He gave the hardest, coldest stare he had ever given in his life. "So leave."

Everything was silent. Clem's eyes were wide and confused. For a minute, he thought she was going to burst into tears, and if she had, he would have let her. He was so full of hatred and anger. He couldn't believe that she would actually go to the limits of spreading lies about him just to be cool, or popular, or whatever the reason was. Who knew how people were going to react to this? They had only just started

The Lopsided Miracle

to react to the paper, but who knew what else she had been telling people.

Everything was so quiet it was scary. Clem could tell. Ben could tell. Ms. Rhodie could tell—that's why she broke the silence.

"What an absolutely fabulous performance, Benjamin! Absolutely award-winning!" She started clapping. Everyone else, relieved with a conclusion to his outburst, started to clap, too. Ben realized that it was only yesterday when everyone was clapping for Clem, but now they were clapping for him. Did that mean that he had done the strong, right thing? Or did that just mean that they liked his performance?

But with one look at Clem's face, he could tell. They both knew it *wasn't* a performance at all.

~

What was she supposed to think?

Ben gave her that long, silent, stony stare that made Clem want to run. She hardly ever ran away from her problems; she usually stayed until things were figured out. But this ... what was she supposed to do? Ben hadn't been acting; the words weren't in the script. They were obviously from his heart—words he had wanted to say for a long time. Clem knew it was true, but the truth was too harsh. For the first time in her life, she wanted to run away.

She got up quickly, fighting back tears while the class's applause was still at a high, and simply walked down the stage, heading towards the auditorium doors.

"Where are you going?" Ms. Rhodie asked, noticing Clem from her peripheral vision.

"I ... I need to go to the ... bathroom," Clem choked out. She blinked and a tear rolled down her cheek. She couldn't believe she was breaking down like this—right in the middle of one of her first days at a new school! But she couldn't help it. She turned and walked as fast as

Emily E. Shipp

she could out of the doors, but as soon as she hit the hallway, she broke out into a run.

She ran all the way down the hall, past all the science and tech labs and a large trophy case. She dashed down the stairs, her feet pounding on each step, making her feel like a thousand pounds, yet she was running like she only weighed five. Her eyes were red and blurry, and she was choking on tears. She couldn't see anything. She was running blindly through the halls. That was all she was doing—running. But she knew, still logical during her mental breakdown, that she needed somewhere to go. She couldn't just run through the halls like a mindless idiot, even though that was exactly what she was doing. So she headed for the bathroom. That way she wouldn't be lying to one of the only teachers she was actually fond of.

She burst through the door, still unable to see clearly, but she *could* still smell. She smelled something. Something disgusting. It was the thick foggy smell of smoke.

Cigarette smoke.

She almost gagged on the awful smell. She had been against smoking all her life. What in the world was going on in here?

She wiped away some tears from her eyes in time to see a girl dressed all in black throw away a cigarette stub in the garbage and shuffle out. Clem knew smoking was against the school policy here—actually, it was against the *law*, but righteous, law-enforcing Clem was too confused to even think about the punk in the bathroom.

Quickly, her eyes filled up with tears again. She ran into the last stall, the stall she had actually been sitting in only a period before. Before, she had been sitting in the stall in fear of Ben's thinking she had said those lies about him to get them published, but now she was there because she was heart-broken.

And worried.

And disappointed.

The Lopsided Miracle

But especially heart-broken. What girl wouldn't be, once she found out the man of her dreams was actually a selfish, little ... *brat*?

After fifteen minutes, the bell rang. About seven other people had come in and out of the bathroom. Clem had cried until all her tears were drained from her body. She had also made a decision about Ben Clavis.

He wasn't as great as she had thought. In fact, she decided that he was incredibly self-involved, and she couldn't believe that he actually had the nerve to say all of those things to her face like that. He didn't have the right! She had done nothing to him but be nice. She even had had a crush on him once, for a very long time.

Yes, she made the decision that she didn't like Ben Clavis anymore—not as a friend and definitely not as a crush!

As she made this decision, this *huge* decision, it felt as though a huge chunk of her had been lifted away, and she was frustrated to admit that it hurt.

At least for now, anyway.

CHAPTER FOURTEEN

The hurt made Clem cry.

Jodie came running into the girls' bathroom a couple of minutes after everyone began leaving Brown Secondary. She had her backpack slung over her shoulders and was yelling Clem's name.

"Clem? Clem? Clem?" she yelled repetitively. She burst open the door to the last stall. She was relieved when she saw that Clem was sitting there.

"Clem!" she gasped, hugging her.

Clem was a little shocked. So what if Jodie was just Jodie? A movie star was hugging her. But it wasn't enough to make Clem forget that the other TV star had just broken her heart into a thousand pieces. "J ... J ...Jodie," Clem's voice cracked.

Jodie just then realized that her guest was sobbing. "Oh, my God! What's wrong?" Her eyes were wide and worried, and her hands were grasping onto Clem's shoulders so hard that her knuckles were white.

Clem looked up at her. She felt so pitiful and small sitting there on a toilet in a strange bathroom in a different school in a foreign country. She felt so out of place for the first time since her arrival.

"Jodie, it was so ..." Her depression was taking over, but then she realized something: She had a choice whether to tell Jodie or not. Yes, she had just had an emotional slap in the face, but to let herself fall apart even more than she had already ... and right in front of a celebrity? She had to pull herself together. She had five more months to stick out.

Unless ...

"I'll tell you later," Clem said. She thought quickly about calling her parents and telling them that she just missed them so much, and she wanted to come home. They would have to send her back, right?

She wiped away her tears and even though more were flowing out, she managed to trudge to her locker, pull out all of the books she needed, and then zip up her backpack and exit the school—all with Jodie following her.

"Clem, are you sure you'll be okay? I mean, I have to go to the set and do scenes for the new episode. Do you want to come?"

Had it been any other time, Clem would have said, "Yes! Of course!" But not today. Today she needed to be alone—anywhere but on the set where she would be surrounded by the last people she wanted to see her cry. She couldn't believe she was going to turn down the offer. She hadn't even really seen the set yet, apart from the day before when she suffered from claustrophobia with reporters all around her. Besides, she had some things she needed to do when she got back to the Clavis's—one thing in particular.

"Sorry, but I think I just need to be alone right now."

"Clem!" Jodie was frustrated, but in a caring way; Clem could tell. "Why won't you tell me what's going on?"

Clem just shook her head. "I said I'd tell you later. When you get back, maybe. Okay?"

Jodie just stood there, open-mouthed and staring. She looked absolutely perfect: perfectly combed hair falling over her shoulders, a perfectly matching outfit, beige corduroy bellbottoms and a beige, white, and tan floral peasant blouse; and, of course, the perfect career. *Maybe if I was like Jodie, Ben would actually like me, not hate me*, Clem couldn't help but think.

She watched as Ryan, Mark, and Ben pulled up in Ben's car. Ryan leaned out the window and smiled at Clem. "You guys want a lift?" he asked, eyes on Clem.

Miserably, Clem turned away. "I'll just take the bus home," she mumbled to Jodie. Then she walked away as quickly as she could, in fear of someone seeing her tear-stained face.

~

The Lopsided Miracle

Jodie hopped in the back with Mark beside her. He grinned at her, for he had a small crush on Jodie, too, now that he had broken up with Marsha.

Ryan turned around and smiled at the two. "Hey," he said, directing his question to Jodie, "What's with Clem?"

Jodie sighed and took some cherry roll-on lip-gloss out of her tan handbag. "That's just the thing—I don't know," Jodie admitted. "She seemed really sad though. I mean, she was crying and everything. I mean, *really* crying."

"Well, didn't you talk to her right before seventh period?" Ryan asked, still twisted in his seat.

Jodie raised an eyebrow. "How did you know that?" she asked.

Ryan shrugged. "You're not the only one who wanted to talk to her," he said.

Mark let out a huge snort of laughter. "Whoo! Ryan's crushin' on the exchange student!" he taunted.

Ryan tried to slug Mark's shoulder, but missed. "Hey, shut up!" he said. A look passed over Jodie's face, but Ben couldn't tell what it was through the rear-view mirror before it disappeared.

"Yeah," Jodie said, scratching her neck, "I did talk to her. But I mean, she seemed fine." Jodie was racking her brain for clues, until all of a sudden, one came upon her so quickly she gasped. "Except ..." she started with a smile.

No one was talking now. Mark and Ryan were now too interested in what Jodie was about to say, so they kept their mouths shut. Ben hoped he didn't look too stressed. What would his friends think when Jodie figured out what he had said?

"Ben!" she shrieked. She looked wide-eyed at her brother, who all of a sudden found the car in front of him very interesting. She leaned forward, so her head was right next to Ben's. "You were in seventh period with Clem ..."

Just deny everything, Ben thought. *She can't blame me yet.*

"Did anything happen? Did Ms. Rhodie say anything?" Jodie asked. Ben sighed a huge sigh—he realized that he had been holding his breath the whole time her eyes had been on him. Unfortunately for him, Jodie looked like she understood the sigh, so he quickly started telling the beginning of a lie.

"No, I don't think Ms. Rhodie said anything. I mean, I don't know though, she might just be going through a ... hormonal imbalance." *What a lame answer!* he thought, but then he decided to lighten the mood by embarrassing his sister. "After all, you little ones are still experiencing changes in the body." He tousled Jodie's hair. She yelped and then quickly fixed it, growling at him. All three boys were laughing.

"Ben!" she said. But after combing her hair out with her trusty, portable pocket-brush, which fit in her handbag, she let out something else. "At least I've gone through changes in the body. You don't have anything."

At this, Mark and Ryan howled even louder. They slapped and pointed at Ben's seat while he turned a deep shade of scarlet.

"Oh, really? And how would you know? So desperate to get a guy, you're spying on me?" Ben glared through the rear-view mirror.

Jodie scowled back at him. "That's disgusting! You're my *brother*, for Heaven's sake, and besides you're so dull that there's absolutely nothing to spy on, anyway. I would know that even if I were a complete *stranger*! I mean, look at your *clothes.*"

"You know what? Put a sock in it!" Ben yelled, barely missing the turn for the road that led to the set.

"I can't! I have to yell directions just so you can get us there without killing us!"

"Jodie!"

"BEN!"

The Lopsided Miracle

"*GUYS!!*" Mark and Ryan screeched in unison. The fighting siblings both turned silent, though still glaring at each other's reflection in the mirror. Jodie finally ended it by tossing her hair and taking out blush from her handbag.

When they finally reached the set, Jodie and Ben were still ignoring each other, but it was Ben who benefited from this. While Mark and Ryan talked with Ben, Jodie was left alone in her trailer to memorize lines before they shot at 4:30.

At 4:00, they all started getting ready. Jodie wished Clem was there so that she could see the real behind-the-scenes action, while Ben was enormously relieved that Clem wasn't there. If she had been, then he and Ryan would probably not be friends anymore. Yes, Ben had found out that Ryan liked Clem *that* much.

"Hey, you know, we haven't practiced in forever," Mark commented while getting into costume. Ben heard him from the other side of the wall in the costume room.

"Yeah, I know," Ben said. Then he grinned to himself. "Hey! I'm free tonight ... you?"

"I think so," Mark said. "I need to make up the time lost with you guys since I was with Marsha. Ryan!" Mark yelled louder. When he didn't get an answer, he asked Ben, "Is Ryan in here?"

"No, I don't think so," Ben said. But just as he said it, Ryan came bursting through the doors of the room.

"Yo!" he yelled, panting and laughing. Ben finished zipping up his pants and came out from behind the wall. Ryan looked as though he had just run a mile in the cold. His cheeks were flushed red and his ears looked about to fall off his head, but as cold as he looked, his expression was gleeful.

"What's up?" Ben asked, pulling on the sleeve of his uncomfortable shirt.

"You ... you ..." He couldn't even talk he was laughing so hard. "You'll never, ever guess what I just saw!"

Emily E. Shipp

Ben shrugged, and Mark finished tying his shoe. Ryan walked over to the two.

"What?" Mark asked. He looked eager; neither Ben nor Mark had ever seen Ryan laugh so hard. This must be good!

"I am the *luckiest* guy ever!" he howled.

"What is it? We have to hurry and go over lines soon!" Mark said, pretending to be practical.

"Okay, okay," Ryan said. He took a few moments to calm himself down, but then he smiled again.

"I just saw *Jodie* in her *trailer*, pretending to ...," he almost couldn't say it because he was laughing again, "... *kiss* on a pillow!"

Mark widened his eyes and screeched, "You're not kidding!" He laughed.

Ben even chuckled a bit, too, but he was sure it would have been funnier if he hadn't already known. Jodie had been pretending to kiss pillows ever since they were little kids. He was surprised he hadn't already told his friends about it. But the other side of him was a little frustrated. After all, she was his sister, and some secrets shouldn't be known to the world. He shook off this feeling, though. It was just a little secret, not anything huge.

"RYAN!" someone screamed. Everyone stopped laughing as Jodie barreled in. She looked like she was about to cry. Ben didn't think it was funny anymore.

"Ryan! How could you just completely intrude on my privacy like that? That was so rude of you, I can't even believe it! You're so immature!" she wailed.

Then Mark piped up. "Don't worry, Jo," he said. "We don't care about you ... kissing pillows." He stifled a laugh. Jodie groaned as tears filled up her eyes.

Ben walked over to her, but Jodie turned away. "Jodie," he whispered, "why are you so mad? It was just an old thing," he said.

The Lopsided Miracle

Jodie whipped up her head. Her eyes looked like fire. "What? No, do you know what I was saying? This is the worst thing to ever happen to me in my life!" Then she ran outside, even though it was freezing cold.

"Oh, man," Ryan said. "I don't know what I did. I just saw her through the window—I didn't know it was such a big deal."

"Come on, you guys," said Mark, repeating what Ben had said. "We don't have to make such a big deal out of it."

But Ben looked to the door without saying anything. Was it just him, or did everything today seem to be bringing someone to tears?

Ben was surprised that Jodie made it through the scenes they did that afternoon. She seemed ready to rip someone's head off—especially Ryan's. Of course, she acted as well as ever on set, but since the scenes they were shooting required Jodie's character to be sour to Ryan's character, Ben didn't think she had to act very much.

Once they were finished, Jodie undressed and got ready to go faster than anyone else. She was finished and ready to head out by the time Ben was just getting started. She walked over to him behind the wall where he usually undressed, not caring whether he was in nothing but boxers and socks. He was her brother, after all.

"Is Ryan or Mark riding home with you?" she asked without smiling or saying a simple "hello."

Ben was about to say something about Jodie invading his privacy while he was standing half-naked, but instead he just shrugged and started pulling his pants on. "Yes. Duh. They came with me here," he said.

Jodie sighed and flicked her hair off her shoulder, pretending not to care. "Fine. I'll catch a ride with Victoria," she said. She turned on her heel and started to walk off.

Ben furrowed his eyebrows and gritted his teeth. He couldn't stand the way his sister was treating him, especially since whatever she was mad about wasn't his fault. "Jodie, wait!" he said. He pulled on his shirt and walked over to her, still in his socks. Jodie turned around and raised her eyebrows as if to say, "Hurry up, I have places to be."

"Why are you acting like this?" he asked. It was bad enough that Clem was probably bawling at his house. Now Jodie, too? Jodie blinked and then sniffed. *Oh, great,* Ben thought, *here come the waterworks ...*

"You don't know why?" Jodie asked, enraged. "I thought Ryan already told you everything! About that stupid pillow and ... me. I hate that! I don't know why I was doing it, because it's a really stupid, childish thing to do, but it's even worse what I said when he was spying on me!" Jodie said, tears blotting her face. She wiped them away with a big sniff, and then looked to the floor. "Of course, he probably already told you about that," she said. Ben stood awestruck. Ryan hadn't said anything about what Jodie had *said*!

"I have to go," Jodie said quietly. "Victoria's going to leave without me." She turned away and walked out as quietly as a mouse, leaving Ben as curious as the cat.

What *had* Jodie said?

He was too curious to wait, so he immediately walked out, leaving his costume behind.

He had to find Ryan—soon!

~

Dear Diary,

It's me again. Today was the worst day of my entire life—ever.

Even worse than when that boy looked up my skirt in the sixth grade.

Even *worse* than when I almost lost Bailey, Brooke, and Beverly at the mall two months ago.

And it was a LOT worse than when mom took away my television for a week so I couldn't watch *The Truth Told by Me,* when I was grounded for not doing my homework.

The Lopsided Miracle

No, today was way, *way* worse.

Clem had her black ink pen poised to write another word when she almost made an accidental line. The front door slammed so hard Clem could have sworn she felt the house shake. She was scared out of her mind it was Ben about to tell her off again, but then she was even more shocked to hear Jodie sobbing, running into her room.

Clem sat still. If she concentrated hard enough, she could hear Jodie mumbling some words, but nothing made sense. It was basically all murmuring. Clem shrugged and was just about to write again when she had a horrible thought.

What if Jodie was mad at her? Clem gasped and dropped her pen on the bed. *Oh My Lord! What if she really is mad at me?* Clem thought, *I mean, I did blow her off today at the car.* She sat, still as a statue, just hoping and praying Jodie wasn't mad at her, but of course, she had the sinking feeling that sitting and wishing would solve nothing. She had to talk to her.

Walking out of the room, she felt guilty at laughing a tiny bit. No matter how hard she tried to stop it, nothing seemed to prevent drama from blooming around the Clavises. Yes, she did have her own problems at the moment, but even though she was learning a lot of new things in Canada, she did know something already—when to be a good friend, and she *wasn't* going to blow off Jodie again.

She knocked on Jodie's door, listening for clues about the waterworks, but Jodie wasn't saying anything anymore. She almost stopped crying altogether when she heard the knocks.

"Who ... who is it?" she asked shakily.

"Hey, Jodie. It's Clem. Can I come in?" *Please don't be mad at me; please don't be mad at me ...*

Jodie sniffled and her bed creaked. Clem guessed she was walking to the door. In a matter of moments, there were foot shadows under the doorway and the knob was turning. Jodie came out, still wearing her clothes from school, but looking an absolute wreck. Clem had an awful déjà vue, thinking about Scarlett on the park bench that day she broke the news her parents were splitting. Clem was a help then—she just hoped she would be now.

"Hey," Clem said.

Jodie sniffed and wiped away some salty tears from her eyes. "Hey," she gulped. Clem looked at Jodie, and Jodie looked at Clem. In just a few seconds, Jodie's tears were streaming again. "Oh, my God," she said. "I'm so sorry, Clem. I'm having a total meltdown …"

"Don't worry," Clem assured her. "You're fine. Believe me. Didn't I just break down today, too?" Jodie snorted and sniffled. Clem honestly couldn't believe a TV star could look so … deconstructed. "Tell me what's wrong," Clem said.

Jodie opened her mouth wide and smiled halfway. She sighed. "Oh … I, well … I don't know. I'm sorry. I just can't tell you yet," she said. Then she wiped away some more tears and looked at Clem again. "But I can tell you this—Ben was no help at all."

It was then that Clem gave out a laugh, but not a hearty, fun laugh. It was a short, loud, mocking laugh. Jodie furrowed her eyebrows and then laughed for real.

Clem thought she would stop, but it had been at least three minutes, and Jodie was clutching her sides with laughing pain. Clem started to laugh, too. "Hey," she asked, "what's so funny?"

Jodie heaved giggles. "I'm sorry!" she wailed, "it's just that we're so pathetic! Both crying like we're three, and we're fifteen!" She giggled. She looked so funny. Her face was still red from crying over something unknown to Clem, but she was laughing as though she had just seen Groucho Marx in his underwear.

Clem couldn't help but agree with Jodie. You know, Ben was just one guy out of a million that she could go out with or have a crush on. Just because he was missing out on her didn't mean she had to sob over it. Clem smiled to herself.

The Lopsided Miracle

Yes, Ben was officially over—and Jodie was officially a friend.

After chatting a little with Jodie and finishing her diary entry, Clem asked to use Jodie's computer. She needed to check her e-mail, because she hadn't checked it since she had arrived in Canada.

Jodie was downstairs watching TV, so she had the room to herself. She was in her new pink pajama pants and matching pink tank-top shirt with her hair in a ponytail. After checking her e-mail, she was going to go straight to bed. She needed to get up early so that she could pick out an outfit that would be stunning enough to revive her reputation. She didn't want to be known as a crybaby to her drama class.

She logged into her screen name as "darlingclem123" at koolmail.com and went straight to her mailbox.

"Whoa!" she said, when she looked at the amount of mail that was hoarding her box. There were twenty messages! She was psyched to see so many, but was a little disappointed when she realized that over half of it was junk mail. She deleted eleven messages and then started to check the other nine.

She rolled her eyes when she saw that the first one was from her new school—Brown Secondary. They were wishing her a "great" new start at Brown. *Oh yeah, just great*, Clem thought. She deleted it. Then she almost jumped out of her seat when she heard a loud *PLING* that burst out of the speaker and a little box popped up on the screen.

"Ah!" she yelped with joy. She smiled from ear to ear. It was Scarlett!

<scarlettflower>: HEY!
<darlingclem123>: HEY 2 U TOO!
<scarlettflower>: I haven't seen you in so long! I didn't think you would ever get on!
<darlingclem123>: Well, I am now.

Emily E. Shipp

<scarlettflower>: How come you haven't replied to my letter?? Did you get the acorns? I thought that was cute.

<darlingclem123>: Yep, I loved everything, but I've just been busy.

<scarlettflower>: How's your new school? OMG, is that guy like a total hottie up close?

Clem snorted and was about to write *life's okay, school's good*, but then remembered that this was her best friend she was talking to—not a new friend like Jodie.

<darlingclem123>: Well, I'm going to tell you everything—do you have time?

<scarlettflower>: Believe me, I have time. There's this TOTALLY hot guy I'm staying with, too!! But he's not in, so until he gets back I'm all ears.

Clem grinned. Yes, this was the Scarlett she knew and was grateful for. She was so relieved to have such a great best friend. Even if they were far away, she knew that she could always rely on Scarlett, and even though this trip seemed to be a total bust now, she would get through it—Ben or no Ben.

She spent the next hour typing as fast as her fingers would fly, telling Scarlett the whole kit and caboodle, from beginning to end. Scarlett only typed three words during Clem's whole story. When she was finally finished, not only did Clem feel relieved and a lot better, but she felt more organized. She felt like now she could start fresh, and better yet, crush on whomever she wanted (as Scarlett put it).

"What fun is it to only have one guy to crush on?" Scarlett typed. Clem agreed.

The Lopsided Miracle

A couple minutes later, Jodie knocked on her door and peeked in. "I need to get on there. Did you have like a million e-mails or something?"

Clem laughed. "Sorry, I was talking to ... someone," she said. "I'll get off." She quickly told Scarlett goodbye and logged off the computer.

Jodie came over as soon as the screen went black. "*Whom* were you talking to?" Jodie asked, handing Clem a glass of water from downstairs.

Clem shrugged and smiled. "A friend," she said. Jodie and Clem said their goodnights and Clem walked out of the room. Then she stopped dead.

There was Ben, going towards her to head downstairs. Normally, Clem would have just stayed right where she was and ogled at him until he was out of sight—but no more. Now he was just the gum on the bottom of her shoe, and at that moment, she needed to scrape it off.

"Hey," she got his attention. He looked at her and then rolled his eyes.

"Oh, it's you," he said. "What do you want?"

Clem walked towards him, clutching her glass of water. "You know," she started. "That was really rude what you did to me today. I *know* that you wanted to tell me that the whole time I've been here, and my question is, why *didn't* you? Are you scared of me or something? Because *I* know a lot of guys who do like me for who I am, and let me tell you, if you didn't like me because I was supposedly a crazed fan, then you are way, *way* off! After what you did to me today, I *strongly* dislike you, and you know what? I can't believe I ever liked you in the first place! I just thought you would like to know that."

Whoa! Clem thought, *I can't believe I just said that!*

Ben, on the other hand, looked like he was going to fall right down the steps. Clem was sure it would have been amusing, but unfortunately, he just shook his head and scowled at her.

Emily E. Shipp

"Well, you know what, Clem? I don't like you either. I *never* liked you, and your little ... *speech* means *nothing to me*!" he yelled.

Clem growled, and without the ability to control herself, she flung her water without one regret at the boy she used to like. "Well, maybe *that* means something to you." She threw the cup on the floor in front of him and tossed her head. "Good *night!*"

~

The next morning, Ben felt like he had a hangover. He had never actually experienced a hangover, but he thought this was probably what it felt like.

He hadn't gotten any sleep at all. His clothes were sticking to him, because he hadn't changed clothes the night before, even though they had been wet. His hair was everywhere, his teeth felt dirty, but—worst of all—inside, he felt dirty, too.

He couldn't believe his conscience had to kick in full gear *now!* His head was spinning so much he was dizzy. The room looked circular and the colors swirled together. He couldn't believe what was happening to him, but before he could stop it, he knew he couldn't turn back.

Why was he feeling so guilty?

"Oh, no!" he said, clutching his head. "I ... I *like* her!"

PART TWO

CHAPTER FIFTEEN

"Remember ... auditions for Cinderella will be at 4:30 tonight! I expect all the drama students to attend for a chance to be in this enchanting play," Ms. Rhodie said enthusiastically.

Fiona must have seen the expression on Clem's face, because she leaned over and whispered, "That's right. Not *everyone* can make it. I'm not worried, though. I always make the lead." Clem looked over as Fiona gave her a devilish grin.

She had decided that she didn't like Fiona very much. Tomorrow was Saturday, and it was only three days until the first day of February. In all the stiff time that Clem had been at Brown Secondary, it seemed that Fiona was always on her tail about something.

"*Brrrrrrrrrring!*" The last bell rang and Clem got out of her seat, deliberately walking past Ben with her nose in the air. She still hadn't forgiven him for the awful way he treated her. She pushed open the doors and walked out to her locker. She started dialing her combination when she was pushed over by a passing klutz.

"Oh, sorry," said the clumsy pupil. He immediately put down his books and started to help Clem pick up her books. Clem looked up to see who her pusher-over was, and she sort of laughed when she saw who it was.

"Hi, Ryan." Clem grinned, picking up her science text.

He grinned back at her. "Hi, Clem. Guess what? I am free tonight. I am going to get pizza. Do you want to come?"

Clem laughed. "Ryan, you don't know how to approach girls very well, do you?" she asked.

He shrugged. "Well, that was my best, so I guess not," he said.

Clem shook her head. She had been getting the feeling that Ryan was crushing on her for a few weeks—maybe longer. "I'm sorry,

Emily E. Shipp

Ryan. I've got an audition tonight for the play," she apologized. Ryan looked a bit disappointed. She quickly recovered the situation. "But hey? You never know when I'll be hungry for a slice!"

Ryan smiled once again and then said a quick goodbye. Clem turned back to her locker, shoving books inside. *Who needs Ben, anyhow? Ryan is just as eligible!* she thought, grinning to herself.

She was going to meet Jodie in the bathroom, so she hurriedly finished packing books into her backpack. As suspected, Jodie was already there when she arrived, applying lip-gloss and checking her eyeliner in the mirror.

"Hey, Clem," she said, smacking her lips together.

Clem tossed her hair back. "Hey, ready to go?" she asked.

Jodie slung her pack over her shoulder and nodded.

As they were walking out of the school, amidst only a few other stragglers, Clem told Jodie about Ryan and the audition.

"Speaking of auditions … what are you going to wear?" Jodie asked, flipping her hair back.

Clem shrugged. "I don't know. What is Cinderella-ish?" she asked. "I don't know … but what about Ryan? Do you think he likes me?"

Was it just Clem's imagination, or did Jodie's smile fade?

"I'll help you pick something out," Jodie said, avoiding the subject. "Oh my gosh! Do you know what else?" Clem shook her head and sat down on a bench, waiting for the bus with Jodie. "You still have to figure out what you're going to wear to the set!"

Clem jumped in her seat once to exaggerate her excitement. "I know, I can't wait!"

And she couldn't. Except for during the newspaper reporter incident, she hadn't even gotten a glimpse at the way it really was on set. She couldn't wait until the next day when she would get a taste!

She couldn't help but think that maybe, one day, she would be discovered as well. These thoughts were foolish, of course, but she

The Lopsided Miracle

couldn't help them. She also started to think about Ryan. What if he did ask her out again? She would be dating a movie star! *That* was something to write home about!

But she wouldn't feel comfortable telling Jodie. If she didn't know better, she would think that Jodie *liked* Ryan ... but Clem knew that was impossible.

Wasn't it?

~

"Ooooh ..." Ben sung into the microphone, which was at that moment turned off.

"Another .... day .... just one more day ... until you come back for me ..." he sang soothingly. Ben strummed his guitar chords while Mark played slowly on the keyboard.

"I've missed you ... for a long while ... don't you see ...?" Ben sang and sang. They hadn't tried playing a slow song before, but this was something Ben had been working on since he had found his ... feelings for Clem. Would she fall for a musician? She had once, maybe she would again.

"Oh, baby! Come back to me-e! Ya know I've loved ya always! Ya know the love is there-e-err!" Ryan sang loudly, drumming a slow beat. Ben played the chords ... slowly and slowly ...

"Another ... day, just one more ..." They all stopped and then sang at various tones the one last word, "day."

The song was over. Ben looked around with a huge smile spread from ear to ear. "Yes!"

"What do you mean, 'yes'?" Mark asked. "Wasn't that more like, 'uh huh! Uh huh'?" he joked.

Ben beamed. "You guys that was ... the best!" He laughed. "What did you think, Ry?"

"It was definitely different for Three's No Crowd," he said. Then he put on a lopsided grin. "But I think it'll be lovely with the ladies."

Emily E. Shipp

Ben was relieved that everyone liked his song. He was afraid that they would hate it, but now that they said they liked it, he could say what he'd wanted to say for the past three weeks.

"I need to sort of talk to you guys about something, like the band," he said, sitting down on the bench, taking off his guitar and setting it down on the top of the table.

"What would you guys think," he started, hoping he was doing the right thing, "about a gig?"

There was silence.

Ben didn't know there could possibly be such a loud silence.

"Sheez, Ben," Mark started, rubbing the back of his neck. "I don't know …"

"I thought we agreed to stay just the way we are now?" Ryan said.

It was the opportunity to make his point. "But why?" Ben asked them. Mark and Ryan both looked at each other. "I mean, why don't we do something to make our music known? Come on! We're already in the TV business … why not give our music a shot?"

There was more silence.

Please, please, please, Ben begged silently.

"Well …" Ryan started. "I don't know, I …" He was trying to be manly and laid-back, but even a great fool could see that he cared—he cared a lot. "I guess we could give it a shot."

Ben looked over to Mark. He just shrugged again and then opened his mouth to speak. "Yeah," he said, trying not to let some disappointment show. "I mean … we could become a real band now that I think about it. Why not?" he said.

They said yes. They said yes! Ben knew he should be relieved, but why did he get the feeling the band didn't want to go through with what he said?

He shook his head and smiled at them. "Cool," he said, taking a swig of pop.

The Lopsided Miracle

He was sure he was doing the right thing. Or, at least he hoped so.

It was for Clem, after all.

~

Clem thought she would be feeling nauseated by now, but actually, she was surprisingly calm. She was only trying out for this stupid play because she had to anyway. She loved drama, but since she was sure Ben was going to get a role, she didn't want to have to spend any excess time with him, if possible. She was wearing her hair up in a bun and a tight, stretchy, brown long-sleeved shirt with regular bell-bottomed jeans. She wore no makeup to look more natural.

She walked into the school after being dropped off by Mrs. Clavis and Jodie (who told her "good luck," but Clem hoped that her luck was just okay—for this play, the smaller role the better) and opened the big wooden doors to the school auditorium.

Surprisingly, it seemed that half the school was there. Of course, Clem knew that had to be wrong because she knew more than half the school must have lives, but now she was just happy that her odds of getting a part were slimmer.

She looked around to see if there was anyone she knew. Luckily, she saw Katherine, swinging her long red hair dramatically over by (and Clem laughed aloud when she saw) Joel Marion, the Swedish exchange student.

She started walking over to the two, passing (to her great disgust) Fiona Whitewaters and her friend Abby practicing a monologue where Fiona was acting as if she forgot something.

She doesn't have to act like it, Clem thought, speeding past her and tapping the flirtatious Katherine on the shoulder.

"Hey, Katherine."

Katherine spun around. Joel smiled. "Oh, 'ello Clementine Greenly." He flashed a smile. Clem had to admit ... he was very cute.

Emily E. Shipp

"Hey, Clem." Katherine looked slightly disappointed that Clem had interrupted their conversation (or more like Katherine's conversation; Joel just stood there and nodded), but she acknowledged her anyway. "I didn't know you were auditioning!"

"I'm in drama ... I have to," Clem said.

Katherine nodded. "Oh, right." She rolled her eyes to herself, clicking her tongue on the top of her mouth. "I knew that!"

Clem smiled. Katherine looked great. She wore her hair down, straight as ever, and looked important. Maybe Katherine would beat Fiona as the lead?

She hadn't realized she had said the last part out loud.

Katherine laughed. "Oh! I don't think so," she said shaking her head. Joel had found a German lad to talk to and had abandoned the two girls. "Fiona may be obnoxious, but she is a great actress. She was the star of the *The Wizard Of Oz* play we did and also *Beauty and the Beast*. She was Belle in that one."

This made Clem mad for some reason. "What? *That* creature? She should have been the beast," Clem said. Katherine laughed at that one. It was hard to hear her, though, over the kids who were practicing their lines. There were so many people, one would think it was an audition for a million-dollar-paying movie job. Right in the middle of Katherine's description of Joel's "perfect" hair, Ms. Rhododendron got up on the stage, looked over the bustling kids who were excited about the auditions, and spoke into a microphone.

"Hello students!" she said cheerily. "Everyone, please take a seat, please take a seat ..."

It wasn't as easy as it sounded. Kids were toppling over each other to get to their friends, and the friends were pushing other kids out of chairs to make room for their friends.

After about five minutes, everyone was seated and ready to hear instructions for the audition. Ms. Rhodie started by welcoming everyone to the audition and telling everyone how exciting it would be to perform this classic play. Then she said what everyone needed to hear. "Now, auditions will run as follows ..." Everyone leaned forward in their chairs. "We will start with the kids in drama right now, starting with the fifth period kids and working up to seventh. Then I will let the kids who aren't in drama try out in alphabetic order. I'm sorry about the inconvenience for you all, but that's just the way I have to set it up for organizational purposes."

"Yes!" Katherine said, "I'm in drama sixth period!"

The wait was awful. It was like waiting in line to get an autograph from a movie star. If Clem had known that it was going to be so slow, she would have arrived forty-five minutes late. Just as Clem was thinking this, Katherine came out waving her hands in the air, beaming.

"Clem! Oh my gosh! How nerve racking! I think I did well, though. Good luck!" she said and raced out the doors like a horse from the Kentucky Derby. A senior wearing an oversized sweatshirt with the school's swim team name on it went up on the stage. She spoke into the microphone. "Seventh period drama, please come backstage," she said, walking to the side to direct everyone where they were supposed to go.

Everyone from Clem's class followed the girl's waving arm until they were backstage sitting in the chairs provided there. Fiona walked past Clem and mumbled, "Good luck ... not."

She wished she could provide Fiona a fork to eat her words.

What had she done to deserve Fiona's catty behavior? Oh, yes. It was because Fiona was jealous that Clem's name had been printed beside Ben's in the paper, and Fiona's hadn't. *She does not know how to handle jealousy*, Clem thought.

Ms. Rhodie came out of a door close to the seats.

"Okay, everyone, we'll go in alphabetical order. Ben Clavis?" Clem had almost forgotten that Ben would be there, but there he was, wearing a sweater and jeans, looking as innocent as possible. Clem saw him glance at her before walking in the door.

Emily E. Shipp

As soon as it shut, people started talking. Well, actually, it was just Fiona; everyone else was practicing pitches of songs and monologues.

"I know that Ms. Rhodie will h*a*ve to cast Ben as the prince, and I'm going to be Cinderella, of course," she said egotistically.

Abby just nodded. "For sure, Fiona," she said, giggling.

Clem wanted to gag.

After about three minutes, Ben came back through the door.

Did he just <u>smile</u> at me? Clem wondered. But she couldn't make sure, because he left the stage without even stopping to talk to anyone.

Ms. Rhodie came out and smiled at Clem. "You're up," she said. Clem got out of her seat and caught a fiery glance from Fiona before walking through the door.

The door shut, but as soon as she was in there, she wished it were open. It was so stuffy and humid, it felt like sweat was hanging in the air. It smelled awful, too, but Clem tried not to concentrate on that.

At the little table in the room, Ms. Rhodie sat down along with two other people she didn't recognize. They were both wearing berets, though, so she supposed they were Ms. Rhodie's friends.

"Clem …" One of the people she didn't know spoke to her, looking down at a clipboard, "Alright, it says here you're going to perform a song?"

"Yes," Clem said. Luckily she had already known a song from Cinderella, one she had memorized a long time ago when she watched the movie nonstop.

"Okay, then. Begin whenever you're ready," Ms. Rhodie said, writing a few things down on the same clipboard the other woman had been holding. Clem wasn't nervous. Maybe it was because she didn't really want to do this with Fiona and Ben in the same play, but that didn't mean she wasn't going to give it her all anyway.

It was deadly quiet, and then she started to sing.

Pure and strong.

The Lopsided Miracle

"I'm as mild and as meek as a mouse ... when I hear a command, I obey ..." her voice pierced the hot air that already felt like a cloak over her head. She remembered that when she was a little girl she would twirl around in circles and sing this song.

She forgot about the judges. She forgot about Ms. Rhodie. She forgot she had been suffocating in that awful prison of a room.

She just sang.

"In my own little corner, in my own little chair, I can be whatever I want to be!" Her voice was as clear as a bell and as soft as an angel's. She smiled and closed her eyes, remembering how the song went.

And she remembered. In fact, she remembered the whole song. She was relieved that she hadn't forgotten it already, but yes, she had remembered, and those few moments that she sang were all hers.

She had never felt so confident!

And then it ended with a long, strong last note.

She opened her eyes.

She lowered her arms.

She saw all of the judges, one by one, their mouths falling open.

And then she heard applause.

"Bravo! Bravo!" The man said, standing up and clapping loudly. Ms. Rhodie was sitting in her seat, her mouth still on the floor, but she was applauding, too. The other woman was practically falling out of her chair in shock. Clem smiled broadly to all of them.

Wow! That felt ... great! she thought, and she knew that it wasn't just the applause she loved.

It was the song she had been singing and that she had felt so free to sing. Maybe singing was her destiny? She was beginning to think it from the way the judges were acting.

"Marvelous! Stupendous!" The man was smiling. "Absolutely ... *perfect!*"

Emily E. Shipp

~

The next day was the day Clem got to see the set.

Ben was looking forward to it, so he could show himself off as the macho-man on set. Well, he hoped he could anyway. He was planning to impress Clem, but he was going to have to do a lot of it to have the nerve to ask her to the Valentine's dance. Mark, Ryan, and Ben had all agreed to be the oddballs and actually take the dance seriously, unlike all the other guys.

Ben just hoped he could get Clem before Ryan did.

No worries, he thought. *With all this lead time, she'll have plenty of time to think of my offer and then say yes!*

He started off the day by taking his regular shower, but he made a big deal of shaving and *not* nicking himself, and putting on a new scent of deodorant. Since he wasn't supposed to do his hair in the morning before time on the set (the hairstylists made sure of that), he just brushed it down, but with a few tricks of the comb, he brushed it over his eyes so it looked rugged—like a surfer's. Of course, he had never even tried surfing before, but Clem had lived in a warmer climate—maybe she liked surfers.

Am I too desperate? he thought to himself. Even *he* knew the answer to that one.

After picking out jeans and a white muscle shirt with a blue plaid, long-sleeved shirt (unbuttoned) on top of it, he was ready to make his approach to Clem. He smiled, giving his ego a boost by thinking he looked like an American Eagle model. Taking a deep breath, he opened the door to his room. He walked down to the kitchen, practically holding his breath—until he saw her.

Was he expecting her to look hideous? She looked better than usual. He tried not to stutter.

"H-hey, Clem," he said. *No!* he thought. *I cannot make a fool of myself. Not today!*

The Lopsided Miracle

To his great disappointment, she didn't even look at him.

"Something wrong?" he asked, pretending to be carefree. He was good at pretending. That was his job, after all.

This time she did look up at him from her magazine. "Ben," she said, shaking her head in a nonchalant manner, "I don't know what you're trying to do, but stop. I'm not as stupid as you may think." And with that, she turned back to the table and kept reading.

So much for the surfing look, he thought, glumly. But then he noticed a very important detail. Clem had not walked out of the kitchen. She was still sitting there, where Ben *had* to sit to eat his breakfast ...

He grinned slyly.

Loudly, he stomped over to the cabinet and pulled down a bowl, clattering it against the glass cabinet door for effect. Then he marched over to the pantry and as loud as he could, grabbed the cereal and forced it down. Marching back to the bowl, he opened the box.

Clank, clank, clank! The cereal bits made a noise in the bowl. Then he took out the milk from the refrigerator. *Glug, glug, glug!* The milk chugged onto the cereal. Then he heard something he thought he would never hear from Clem ever again.

A chuckle!

He quickly spun around. It was true! There she was, smiling over her magazine. He knew it wasn't a funny article, either. He prayed his relief didn't show.

"What's so funny?" he asked.

Clem bit her lower lip. "Nothing," she said, trying not to smile. "You just remind me of Stephen and his awful habits, too."

Then she got up and left.

Stephen? Ben thought. Questions were suddenly racing through his brain. *Who's Stephen? Is he an old boyfriend? A new one? Does he go to Brown? Do I know him? Is he from South Carolina? Will he hunt me down and punch me if I ask Clem out?*

He furrowed his brow.

Emily E. Shipp

This is harder than I thought, he thought to himself. Since she was out of the room and his first impression hadn't exactly impressed her that morning, it was time for plan B.

He set down his cereal bowl.

Walking back upstairs, he noticed that Jodie's door was closed while Clem's was open. He hadn't seen Clem anywhere else, so he knew she must be with Jodie.

Perfect.

He knocked, more politely than usual. Even Jodie must have noticed the difference.

"Mom?" she called through the door. Ben closed his eyes tight, wanting to punch his "darling" sister.

"It's Ben," he said through clenched teeth. He tried to open the door, but it was locked. Another perfect opportunity. To make up for the womanly trait Jodie just used on him, he turned the knob twice to the right and then pushed hard to the left. The door unlocked.

"Ben!" Jodie yelled from her closet, coming out with Clem following close behind. "That was locked!"

"I know, but I needed to get in. I just used my shoulder to push it open," he said. *No stuttering*, he complimented himself.

"Ben," Jodie said, her eyes half-closed, as if she were giving a thousand-year-old lecture. "I'm not stupid. I know the door unlocks if you do the little turn thing. Stop trying to be... *strong*, or something."

Ben blushed.

"Don't have to be so jealous, *no* mo-jo," Ben said.

Jodie pointed to the door. "Both of you get out! You *and* your lame cracks!"

Clem laughed at Jodie's side. Ben blushed even harder. He had to do something before all of his chances fell right out the window.

"I just wanted to know if you needed a ride to the set," he said casually. *Please say yes ...*

The Lopsided Miracle

"Um, *no* thank you. Mom is going to take us. This is supposed to be an *enjoyable* day for Clem. We don't need you stinking up the beginning."

To make matters worse, Ben could tell Clem wanted to say the same thing. Nothing was going right. If he didn't know any better, he would say that Ryan could just have Clem for all the luck he was having, but he wasn't going to give up that easily.

"Fine," Ben said, turning around. "Have fun riding in the loser cruiser."

He walked away and Jodie slammed the door on his back. Plan A *and* plan B had both backfired. He was going to have to think up a plan C ... before Ryan could call the target.

~

"You remember Victoria?" Jodie smiled her winning smile in Victoria's direction.

"I can never forget a pretty face!" Victoria chimed in.

Clem smiled sheepishly. "Thank you, ma'am," she said politely.

"Oh! Southern manners! I love it." Victoria grinned, setting Jodie down in the chair with the plastic cover on it.

"You can sit over here, Clem," Jodie offered. Clem backed up, but then felt someone sit down quickly, making her fall into his lap.

"Ah!" she squealed, looking around. She saw Ryan's smiling face looking back at her. She laughed as she got off his lap. "Hello to you, too," she beamed. She looked back at Jodie, still laughing. To her great surprise, Jodie looked as giggly as a rock. But only for a second, then she was smiling again.

"Ryan, you're such a kidder," she said sarcastically.

A few moments later, they were joined by Mark and, to Clem's disappointment, Ben.

Emily E. Shipp

Something fishy had been going on lately involving him. He was being so ... nice to her. She thought she was imagining things, until that morning when she finally knew something was up.

Was it a bet? She thought it might be. She could just see a couple of his lame-o friends (who weren't Mark or Ryan) betting Ben he could get Clem to fall head-over-heels for him again in less than three weeks or something just as ridiculous. She only knew one thing, and that was that she wasn't going to fall for it.

After Jodie was finished with her makeup, she and Clem went down to wardrobe, where they met a young woman with a headset on, picking out outfits.

"Oh, hi, Jodie hun!" she said. She seemed about nineteen and looked like she was a beauty pageant queen. She smiled and handed Jodie a pair of absolutely radical jeans and an awesome midriff shirt that matched the seams in the pants. Clem almost doubled over with jealousy.

"This is for the first couple of scenes today, and for you to keep. I talked Joe into letting me buy it for you since I know you just loved it when we were looking at things for this new episode."

Jodie beamed. "Oh, my God, thank you so much, Candice!" she yelled, squeezing Candice around the middle.

Candice laughed. "Well, go put it on! We're starting the shooting in an hour," she said, walking to the boys' part of the room.

Clem frowned. She didn't think Candice even noticed her, but she tried to tell herself that Candice wasn't the one she needed to impress. It was Joe Carton, the one who would have to discover her!

She sighed.

"Can you believe this? These shoes are outrageous!" Jodie said, going behind a changing stand.

Clem tried not to let her jealousy show. "Yep, totally cool," she said, eyeing the door in case Mr. Carton decided to make an

The Lopsided Miracle

appearance. A couple of minutes later, Jodie came back out from the stand, looking like a movie star.

"Wow!" Clem said. "I wish I was in your shoes." Then realizing the two meanings of this phrase, she laughed. "I mean, I wish I was you right now."

"Phsh." Jodie made a noise through her lips. "It's not all that great. I mean, the clothes are the best part of the whole thing. Now, I have to go over my lines for the first couple scenes. Help me?"

Clem shrugged, feeling ugly next to Jodie. "Sure."

They practiced for a long while, until Jodie had memorized everything. Clem had to admit that acting was not all glamorous; all those lines were almost painful! But once they were finally done, Jodie suggested they take a look in her trailer since Clem hadn't gotten to see it before.

They walked across the cement set outside, where the sun had started to peek out from the clouds. It was still pretty cold outside, but at least the sun would make things cheerier.

Jodie pushed open the door to her trailer. Clem's eyes widened when she walked inside. "This is so cool! I just can't get over it," she said.

Jodie smiled. "Yeah, I like it, too." Before they could even sit down on the couch, though, someone knocked at the door and barged in.

It was Ben, of course.

"Hey, Clem! Hi, Jodie," he added quietly. "Do you guys wanna play Crazy Eights? Mark and Ryan are both down there."

"Oooh! Sounds fun!" Jodie piped. "Come on, Clem!"

Clem decided it would be a whole lot easier to avoid situations with Ben if she told Jodie of her strong disliking for him. But she felt she couldn't do that, since she had already told Jodie that she didn't like him. "Um, maybe I'll join you guys later. I want to walk around the set some more." Jodie didn't look too disappointed. Clem wondered why.

Emily E. Shipp

"Well, okay! We're shooting in about twenty minutes, though, so hurry back!" and before Ben could even say anything, Jodie shoved him out the door and it closed behind them.

"Hmm ..." Clem wondered. She peeked out the window at the two who were walking away. Ben was trying to loosen his grasp from Jodie, and was having a lot of luck until Jodie said something to him, almost regrettably, with sad eyes. He stopped then, turned around, and exchanged some words with his sister for about two minutes until Ben nodded, and they started walking away again.

Something had changed Ben's mind. Clem raised her eyebrows and rolled her eyes. That was *okay* with her—she didn't want to be around him anyway!

She left the trailer when they were gone and started looking for Joe.

~

Ben couldn't believe what his sister had just told him.

Jodie liked *Ryan*!

All the time that she had known Ryan, she had liked him, and that was why she was so angry when he saw her kissing her pillow—because she was pretending to kiss him!

That's why she wanted to leave Clem behind—because she wanted things to be like they used to be. She hadn't told Clem about her crush, either. No one knew—except for Ben.

Ben wanted so badly to tell Ryan, but Jodie made him swear to secrecy, and Ben had been a jerk enough lately—he wasn't about to betray his sister.

The whole time they were playing Crazy Eights, Jodie acted like she normally did towards Ryan, but to Ben it seemed like the longest game he had ever played. Not only was this weird news—it benefited him, too!

The Lopsided Miracle

If he could get Ryan and Jodie to go to the dance together, then Clem was all his!

That day, they shot the entire episode and the whole time, Ben was hardly thinking about acting—he was thinking about a way to get Ryan and Jodie together without breaking his promise. Clem was off to the side, intrigued by the action on the set, and also with Joe Carton. Ben knew why. Who didn't want to become famous?

It was pretty late in the afternoon when they were finally ready to go. Ben's plans were hatching in his head, and he couldn't seem to think about anything else.

The first of the month was coming up. At that time, he would have two weeks to convince Jodie to go with Ryan and get up the nerve to ask Clem to the dance. Not to mention that he had already said something about a gig for his band. Little did he know that February was going to be the craziest month of his life.

CHAPTER SIXTEEN

February was finally here.

It was Monday: the day all the drama kids had been waiting for. It was the day the cast for *Cinderella* was to be posted on the school bulletin board. Katherine met Jodie and Clem outside the school before the doors were even opened.

"Ah!" she squeaked. "I am *so* excited! I hope I make it!" Clem grinned, silently hoping that she *hadn't* made it. Over her shoulder, Jodie pointed to a group of girls with Fiona in the middle.

"Look, it is miss I'm-the-best-so-you-don't-have-a-chance," Jodie said, smirking.

"I don't know what her problem is," Clem said. "I mean, even when I was trying out for the play, she tried to give me a hard time. She must be totally obsessed with Ben because she's still mad at me about that fake article."

"I know," Katherine said. "I don't understand why she thinks she's queen of the world, *or* why she's so popular. She only has that *one* group of friends, and I don't even think they like her all that much."

Just then, the bell rang and kids started swarming inside. As Clem bent down to pick up her backpack, someone brushed against her shoulder, knocking her to the ground.

"Don't even bother looking at the cast, Clem," Fiona said, kicking Clem's backpack. "I know I made the final cut anyway, and losers like *you* don't ever! So," she held up her hand and walked away with her final words, "later, loser."

Clem got up and slung her backpack on her shoulder.

"Urg!" she grumbled. "I hate her!"

"We *will* make the cut, Fiona!" Katherine yelled to her back. "And when we do, we'll see who the loser is!"

Jodie opened her mouth in a broad smile and slapped Katherine's hand. "Hey, that was pretty good," Jodie complimented Katherine.

Katherine shrugged and started walking inside along with everyone else. "I guess, but what if I don't make it now? Then she'll never let me live it down."

They all went straight to the postings, but had to wait for about five minutes just to see the board. There were so many people there! Some came out of the swarm with happy smiles on their faces, while others looked about to cry, but there was one look that Clem would never forget. As Fiona walked up to the board— people, of course, giving her a path to walk through—she looked like a queen. Clem was expecting Fiona to catch her eye and give her an evil smile of defeat, but instead, something else happened.

Her eyes widened, she sucked in her breath, and gasped.

"Oh, my God!" she shrieked, and then, with a dramatic hand on her forehead, she fainted.

And she wasn't acting.

Everyone who was around the board quickly forgot about the roles posted and dropped to the floor to help Fiona, except for Clem, Jodie, and Katherine, who were still interested to see the posting.

And Clem knew right away why Fiona fainted.

At the very top of the list there were the words that made Clem's mouth drop to the floor.

Cinderella—Clem Greenly.

~

Ben arrived just in time to see a nurse on the floor with Fiona, and Clem walking away from the board, looking dumbstruck. Something was up. He quickly dashed over to the board to see what it was.

Yes!

His luck was finally turning around! It was way too good to be true. He was the prince! But even better, *Clem* was Cinderella! No

The Lopsided Miracle

wonder Fiona almost had a heart attack. She hated Clem's guts and kissed up to Ben. Not only that, but Fiona was cast as the ugly and evil stepmother!

Ryan walked up and saw what Ben was gawking at.

"Oh man!" He said sarcastically, "I am no longer your friend."

"What do you mean?" Ben said, pretending to be clueless.

"What? You get to make out with Clem! And you're *supposed* to!" Ryan pointed to the cast.

Ben wanted to fly. "I'm not making out with her. I don't want to anyway, remember? Besides, and thank goodness, it's only a little kiss at the end." This brought his spirits down a bit, but they were his own words—he didn't have to believe them. He could believe Ryan's instead.

"I wish I had tried out. I couldn't, though. My mom said she would never get to 'see me.' Like she ever does anyway. I'm always out as it is," he said grumpily.

"Don't worry about it," Ben said. "There's always …"

"The dance, I know." Actually, the dance wasn't what Ben had in mind, and he was slightly put out that Ryan remembered it. "Speaking of that, I have to ask her. Luckily, she seems to be getting over you!" He smiled. Ben tried, but he really couldn't.

The play had seemed great, but Clem wouldn't really want to be there. It would all be fake. Ryan was the lucky one: He would get to go with Clem to the dance and get a real kiss from her.

But then Ben remembered his plan about Jodie.

"Yeah, Ryan, but you know, what about Jodie? I think she was really wanting you to ask her."

Ryan almost laughed aloud. "Oh, get real, man. She's never once showed signs of wanting to be with me! Besides, Clem is a once in a lifetime opportunity."

That's why I want her! "Yeah, but …"

Emily E. Shipp

The bell rang for class to begin. Ben hadn't even put away his books yet.

"See you around, Ben," Ryan said, waving happily.

Unfortunately for Ben, his emotions had flip-flopped during their conversation. He sighed and just started walking to class. Mrs. Walsh would be mad that Ben was carrying around his backpack, but oh well. Ben was mad, too.

When he opened the door to the class, it was as usual, except that everyone was gabbing about the play. Mark was there, too, waiting for him to arrive. Fiona was the only one who wasn't there that morning, and he heard some chatter that she might not be there at all for the rest of the day—since she was so crushed by the judges' choice of cast.

Even Mark noticed her disappearance. "Have you heard about Fiona?" he asked curiously.

"Yeah, I was there," Ben said.

Mark rubbed his hands together. "I can't believe it! She didn't get the lead! Not that I really care, but she always gets the lead ... I mean, every time!"

"You think I didn't know that? I am in every play with her!" Ben said snorting. He truly didn't like her very much, and he hated to admit that he was afraid that he would have had to kiss her instead of ... someone else. "Can we not talk about Fiona?" Ben asked before Mark could ask another question.

He shrugged. "Sure," he said. Even though the bell had already rung, Mrs. Walsh was still not in the room. No one else really seemed to notice.

"We're still having practice tonight, right?" Ben asked.

Mark nodded. "Yep. Oh, and I forgot to tell you ... I have really been thinking about that gig idea of yours, and it actually might not be so bad."

"What? I thought you liked it from the beginning!" Ben said.

The Lopsided Miracle

"Well, I had my doubts, but really. I mean, none of us has a date for the dance yet, and what, besides chocolate, gets to a girl's heart better than music? We'll all have offers by the end of the night! Well, except for Ryan, who will already be fighting off the guys for Clem."

Ben was stung. "Oh, yeah. You don't really think he'll ask her, do you?"

"Well, yeah.—" But then Mark stopped talking. He looked at Ben curiously. "You don't ... *like* her, or something ...?"

"What!" Ben pretended to be enraged. "Oh, come on, Mark. Start taking medication! The girl is, like, the complete opposite of me! Ryan can have her for all I care." Maybe he had said too much. He only knew one thing right then, and that was that he had to be more careful of what he said—or someone might know about his bite by the love bug. "Besides, there's that new club that just opened, for teens, you know? What's it called? Club ..."

"The Circle Club? Yeah, I heard that place was jammin'! We should try to get a gig there."

"That was my point," said Ben. "Let's talk to Joe after we get out of here. Maybe he could put in a good word for us there."

After school, the three guys headed to Ben's car so they could go to the set, where Joe said he would be that day.

"The Circle Club?" Ryan was trying to remember the name. "I don't know. I've never heard of it before."

"That doesn't matter. The point is if we talked the manager into giving us a job there this weekend, we could be on our way. Think about it. You could get Clem twenty times easier this way!" Mark put in.

Not if I can help it, Ben thought to himself. Unfortunately, Ryan was actually taking this seriously.

"Good idea," he said. Ben could tell Ryan was thinking it over.

"Let's go," said Ben, trying to distract his thoughts. "Joe will be gone by the time we get there."

Emily E. Shipp

Luckily, no one said anything sarcastic or annoying and obediently got into the vehicle. Ben closed the door and pumped up the radio, still trying to stray Ryan's thinking away from Clem.

"*Suga ... suga ... suga ...*" some girl was singing in a low voice to a slow tune. Ben changed the dial.

"*WHOA!!!!!!*" a very *bad* band was screaming to off-tempo drums. Ben quickly changed it again.

"Do you want the best of the best? Come to Jack's Auto Park ..." Ben was about to change it again when Mark, who was sitting up front, turned it off.

"Hey!" Ben said.

"I can't listen to anything. I'm shaking for God's sake," he said. Ben observed his hands when he stopped at the red light. They were.

"What are you so hyped about? We're just going to go in and ask for help for the band, then make a quick stop by the club to interview."

"Wait!" Ryan cried from the back seat. "We're going to the club *today*? Shouldn't we get our stuff or a tape of us playing or something?"

Ben tightened his grip on the steering wheel. He hadn't thought about that, but he had a point. "Crap," he mumbled under his breath. "Ok. Fine. We'll talk to Joe, and then we'll meet at the club at 7:00. How's that?"

Everyone agreed to the plan, but as soon as they did, Ben could feel the tension in the air. Mark started jiggling his foot, and Ryan started whistling to an old tune that no one could identify. Ben broke the speeding limit twice, and both times Mark yelled, "What are you trying to do? Get a ticket?" Ryan started tapping his fingers together. Ben's eyes were getting wider and wider.

"This is stupid." He pulled over onto a gravel spot on the shoulder of the road, swinging the car out of the traffic and swinging everyone in the car with it. Then, once everything came to a halt, Mark started shouting again.

The Lopsided Miracle

"Ben! You *moron*! You could have gotten us killed!" His arms flailed in every direction.

"Shut up!" Ben said. He closed his eyes and sighed. "Look," he said, "we've got to stop doing this. We're acting like ... girls. I mean, we know how to interview to do something, so why are we so nervous ... right?"

Ryan cleared his throat. "Duh. We're nervous because we're not just talking in front of a camera. There won't be any bloopers now. This is for real and, let's face it, everything will be screwed if we mess up."

Ben turned back to the road. "I get what you're saying, but I swear if you don't stop tapping your fingers together, I will have to kill you."

~

"Clem! It's your mother on the phone!" Mrs. Clavis yelled up to Clem's room. Clem grinned, running downstairs.

"Thank you, Mrs. Clavis," she said sweetly, grabbing the phone and holding it up to her ear.

"Mom?" she said hopefully.

"Clem!" Mrs. Greenly said on the other line.

"Mom!" Clem smiled. "Oh, I'm so glad you called!"

"I was missing you too much," said Mrs. Greenly. "Besides, I haven't heard anything from you lately. I have only received one letter, and that was quite a while back."

"Sorry, Mom," Clem said, sliding herself onto the couch in the living room. "I've been really busy."

Mrs. Greenly laughed. "Really? Well, the twins are napping, so I have time to talk."

Clem bit her tongue in a broad grin. "Well, narrowing it down," she looked to the left and to the right, "Ben Clavis is really a jerk, but Jodie Clavis, his sister, rocks." She sighed. "And then the newspaper made a fake remark that I was Ben's girlfriend, and I tried out for the

Emily E. Shipp

school play against the girl who was mad at me because she liked Ben and thought the paper was telling the truth. Then I found out I made the star role, Cinderella, and Ben made the prince, so now I don't even want to be in it, but I know you wouldn't want me to quit. Would you?"

There was silence on the other line. "My goodness," her mother finally said. "You have been busy! You never told me you were in the newspaper ..."

"Mom!" Clem said. "That's beside the point. Didn't you hear me say that I was going to be the star of the school play with the guy I *hate?*"

She laughed again. "Yes, I heard that part, too. I thought you liked this guy. What made you change your mind?"

Clem rubbed her temples. "It's kind of a long story, Mom."

"I have time, dear," she said.

Clem licked her lips. "Then I'd better tell, huh?" she asked.

"You'd better. Besides Scarlett, whom I am just presuming you've talked to already, I am your main source of relief."

Clem laughed. "Thanks, Mom," she said quietly.

"It's my job, dear."

Clem heard rustling on her mother's side of the line. Then she heard a familiar voice. Her mother talked for a minute to the voice, and then started talking to Clem again. "Bailey wants to talk to you," she said.

Clem's eyes squinted with joy. "Sure," she said. The phone was quickly transferred to Bailey, Clem's favorite eight-year-old.

"Clem?" she said happily.

"Hi, Bailey."

"Hi, Clem! What's going on? Are you having fun there? Is it cold? Can you go sledding?"

Clem laughed. "I probably could go sledding," she said, "but I haven't tried it yet."

The Lopsided Miracle

"You're nuts. Going all the way to a cold place and not even sledding."

"Oh, Bailey." Her eyes turned sad. "Maybe I am nuts. Why did I leave you? I'm just putting more stress on myself." She said the last part softly.

Bailey was quiet for a minute. "No," she said, "you left to relieve the stress of someone else."

Is this coming from my eight-year-old sister? Clem wondered. "That's very insightful," Clem commented.

"Thank you," Bailey said, "but I'm not finished. Clem, I've known you my whole life. I love you more than anyone, almost more than Mommy or Daddy, and in all that time, I just knew one thing. You're the bravest, coolest, most awesome person I know. When you said you were going, I was pretty sad, but ..." She paused. Clem's eyes dampened with tears. "You can be that awesome, cool, brave person no matter where you go. I should know. You're the best sister ever."

Clem started crying. "Oh ... oh my gosh, Bailey." She wiped away some of her tears on her sleeve. "*You're* the best sister ever. Please, don't ever forget that."

"I won't," Bailey said. "By the way, are there any souvenir stores there?"

~

Ben opened the door to his house to the smell of roast beef on the stove. He would have to make a quick escape—he would never get to leave the house if he was lured by that smell. Walking upstairs, he ran into Clem who was wiping her eyes. She was crying.

Do it! he screamed inside. *Ask her!*

"Hey, Clem," he said. He pretended he had just noticed her tears. "Is ... is something wrong?"

Emily E. Shipp

She looked up at him, glaring. "Sentimental stuff. Nothing you could understand." Then she walked into her room, shutting the door behind her.

Ben closed his eyes. Why did he have to be such a jerk before? And why couldn't she see how hard he was trying to make up for it?

He swallowed hard, his Adam's apple going up and down. Walking into his room, he changed quickly into some newer jeans and a navy blue T-shirt. Running his fingers through his hair, he approved his outfit and picked up his guitar from the corner of his room. Then, holding his nose, he left the house and hopped into his car again. Miraculously, the smell of roast beef hadn't been a problem for him.

He squinted into the day, which was beginning to become night. His car rolled along the streets. Unfortunately, there was traffic everywhere he looked, and at one point, he was stuck in bumper-to-bumper traffic in the same spot for seven minutes.

It was 6:30 at the moment he finally moved. He prayed he wouldn't be late for the audition. Joe had finally agreed to come along with them to check it out, and Ben didn't want to let anyone down. He looked around the car for his cell phone so he could call to see where the guys were and if they were stuck in the same traffic, but he couldn't find the phone anywhere.

"Oh, shi—"

Beep!

He looked over to his left. Miraculously, the Circle Club was on the next turn, and traffic was finally moving faster!

"Thank the Lord!" he said, turning into the club's parking lot.

Surprisingly, for a Monday night, the place was a zoo. It was very nice, with its glass doors and modern exterior ... and the band that was playing was obviously very good.

The Lopsided Miracle

Right next to him, a car pulled up. It was a little sports car with a sleek exterior. Joe stepped out. "Hello, Ben, good to see you're on time. Where are Ryan and Mark?"

"I don't know. I don't have my cell phone with me, or I would have called them. We're early, though, right?"

"Yes, it's unacceptable to be late." He locked his car by pushing a button on his key ring. "And I had to be here to make sure you didn't make a fool of yourself. Come on! We'll wait for them inside."

It was times like this when Ben truly did not like Joe very much. He treated Ben more like a dog than a person when he wanted Ben to make a good impression.

Two buff-looking men with police attire guarded the doors. Ben walked right past them, and Joe started scanning the room.

"Stay with me, Ben. This place is a nuthouse."

Ben looked at him with one eyebrow up. "Joe, I'm not three. I can handle myself." Just then, a girl about his age, wearing an extremely low-cut shirt, came up to him.

"Hey, big guy," she said, doing a funky shoulder motion, "don't I know you from somewhere?" A group of girls giggled behind her. Of course she knew him. He was on TV for goodness sake.

"Frankly, I haven't seen you anywhere in my life. If you'll excuse me, I have business to attend to."

Whoa! he thought. *What am I doing?!*

The girl looked at him oddly and huffed, turning and walking away to some other guy by the bar.

Ben couldn't believe he had just blown off a gorgeous girl. Were these the beginning effects of a serious crush? Not being able to look at other people at all? Personally, he wished it would go away. As he was just thinking that, he saw two people he knew doing what he wished he could have done with that girl.

Emily E. Shipp

Mark and Ryan were dancing crazily with two other people who each resembled the girl he had talked to. Ben widened his eyes and started walking towards them.

"Yo!" he yelled. "What are you doing?" Ryan didn't hear him at all, but Mark stopped immediately. The girl leaned over and gave him a kiss on the cheek before walking over to her group of friends who were all dancing in another part of the room.

"What are you doing? I thought you weren't here yet!"

"Well, you know, I thought I would have some fun before we had the interview, and believe me, we were having some *fun!*"

"Did you even catch her name?" Ben asked.

Mark frowned. "Does that really matter?"

Ben wanted to hit him. He also wanted to hit Ryan, who had just finished dancing with the girl and was now signing a piece of paper for her. He supposedly liked Clem a lot—yet he was dancing with another girl. Was Ben just an idiot? Or was Ryan the loser?

"Ryan! Get over here!" Oh no. Had he said it too loudly? They had now caught the attention of other people around them. The music hadn't stopped, but everyone who was standing near them had heard. All of a sudden, they had people swarming all around them.

"Oh, my God!" Girls' cries and screams surrounded them. Paper and napkins were being flailed at them to sign. Ryan was trying to fight his way through the crowd.

"Let me out! Let go!" Ben and Mark were yelling. People were trying to get their arms out to touch them. Just as they thought they would have to actually autograph their way free, the two guards who were at the door came bursting through the crowd, picking up Ben and Mark like they were as light as pillows. They were raised above the crowd, which was now following the guards. They heard a door open and close. Then they were set down on chairs.

Ryan was already there, with lip prints all over his face. "Whoa," was all Ryan could say.

The Lopsided Miracle

Joe was in the room with another buff man, this one wearing a business suit. Both were smiling.

"This, Mr. Pitching, is the band," Joe said.

Mr. Pitching put his face right up to Ben's, so Ben had to draw back in his seat. "I thought I knew these kids," he said. He then directed the conversation straight to the three. "TV show kids, right?" he asked. They all nodded in unison. "Sounds good. Got a name?"

"Three's No Crowd," Ben blurted.

Mr. Pitching thought this over. "Three's No Crowd," he repeated. "Sounds good. 'Music tonight performed by Three's No Crowd.' I like it."

The three youths smiled. "Sweet," Ryan said. Ben could tell Ryan wasn't thinking about the audience, but about one special person he would have an opportunity to impress. Ben knew, disappointedly, that Ryan probably could do a lot of impressing, too, since he was the drummer.

"But, you don't have the job that easily. You brought instruments, I guess?" Mr. Pitching asked.

"Yeah!" Mark said. "We'll go get them!"

Wow, Ben thought, getting up out of his chair. *This is sweet!*

The three walked out to their cars (with the police guards of course), while Joe and Mr. Pitching talked about advertising the band. Mark and Ryan had broad grins on their faces.

"Can you believe it? We're going to be famous!" Ryan exclaimed.

"Ryan, we *are* famous," Mark said.

"Oh, right."

Ben rolled his eyes and unlocked his car, taking out his guitar. Mark got his keyboard, which was held in a long, black case. Ryan said he was going to use the drums the club provided.

Walking back in, they decided to perform two songs: Ben's song, the one he had written for Clem, though no one else had to know it, and

Emily E. Shipp

another rock song that Ben hated to play since it was so hard but Ryan and Mark loved because it sounded so cool.

The guards led them back inside, but this time, they were led into a room in the very back of the club that read "staff only" on the door. From its location at the place, it looked like just a janitor's closet or some such thing, but when one of the guards opened it, all three of the boys' eyes almost popped out of their heads.

It was an auditorium, not as tall as it was long. There was a modeling runway and a stage for bands, Ben supposed. Mr. Pitching took out the club drums for Ryan to use and set them up on the stage. Joe Carton flicked on the lights facing the stage, and they were so bright that all three guys had to hold up their hands to their faces.

"This is how bright the lights on the outside stage are," Mr. Pitching said, "so if you're going to work for us, get used to it."

The band members looked at each other.

Everyone started plugging things in and testing things out. They all felt the heat.

"Are we going to do this *today*?" Joe asked testily.

Ben sighed. He pretended not to be nervous, but now the pressure was on. If they messed up, they wouldn't get the job. That was that.

"Okay," Ben whispered. "Let's go."

CHAPTER SEVENTEEN

"So anyway, Abby, did you hear about the Circle Club thing on Friday? I am *so* going. Ben's band is playing there! I didn't even know he was in a band. That is so cool," Fiona said, tossing her hair.

It's weird how much she sounds like me a couple months ago, Clem thought. In her thoughts, she tried to emphasize the "months" part. She couldn't believe Ben. She, of course, had already known he was in a band, but she couldn't believe he was flaunting it so. There were posters all over the walls reminding people to go to the Circle Club because "three fellow members of our school community will be playing in their band there."

Clem knew she wouldn't be caught dead there.

She was sitting still in her chair, reading and waiting for Ms. Rhodie to arrive and start the drama class. Of course, Ben was sitting in the chair right in front of her (another mystery) and talking rather loudly to some of the other people who made the play.

"I wasn't nervous at all. It was great playing there, after all. There were tons of people there, and they were all watching us play for the first time, and then we were swarmed by fans." Clem tried to keep reading. "It was crazy. Not to mention they gave us the job easily. It was nothing, really."

Clem slammed her book closed, and taking her backpack, she got up and walked to another seat, a lot farther away from Ben's chair.

She wanted to get away from him.

"Clem wait!" someone called after her. Clem rolled her eyes but smiled. She stopped and turned around to face him.

"Hi, Ryan." She grinned.

"Hi," he said. "You busy tonight? You owe me one."

Emily E. Shipp

Clem thought about it. She didn't have play practice, and she had finished all her homework in study hall. Why not? It wasn't as if she had anything better to do ... and besides, her mother wasn't there to tell her no. "Nope," she said, "I'm free as a bird."

Ryan looked extremely relieved.

"Cool. Pick you up at 6:00?"

Clem pushed her tongue behind her teeth. She had discovered this method of smiling a while back—it was a sexy look. "I can't wait," she said, and as he turned and walked away, she stared at her locker.

She was going to go out on a date with a TV star—so why wasn't she happier?

~

Ben felt like an idiot.

He had scared her away! He wanted to impress her with his talk of the band and their tryout, but no. Instead, he had looked like an egotistical brat.

Not to mention that half the stuff he was blabbering on about wasn't even true! He *had* been nervous, even though he said he hadn't been. Tons of people *weren't* watching them, only Joe Carton and Mr. Pitching. Yes, fans *had* swarmed them, but it had not been a pleasant experience, and they had not gotten the job easily. Actually, the band *and* Joe had to practically beg Mr. Pitching to let them perform because the last song they played had been so incredibly off-key.

The worst part was it felt to Ben as if she knew he was lying.

Finally, Mr. Pitching had agreed to let them play because of the exposure it would give to the club, and only if they practiced their music. When Mr. Pitching had mentioned publicity, Ben cringed, remembering Mrs. Queenly's talk to him and his sister about their publicity. Come to think of it, that stupid speech was what got him into this awful position in the first place!

The Lopsided Miracle

He shook off those thoughts, making a vow to himself that he would try to let the past be the past, and caught up to Ryan who was walking with his chin held high down the hall.

That can't be good, Ben thought.

"Hey!" he yelled. "Ryan!"

Ryan turned around immediately. "Oh, hey! Guess who's in da *house?!*" he asked excitedly.

Ben stopped abruptly. *This really can't be good*, he thought. "What?" he asked.

Ryan obviously hadn't caught on to the unenthusiastic tone in Ben's voice. "I just got a date with the exchange student!" he said, smiling and waving two thumbs up and down wildly.

"Please tell me you're talking about the Mexican exchange student," Ben said with a slight begging tone in his voice.

Ryan didn't catch on to this, either. He was still smiling. "Nope!" he said. "The American one. Clem! She said yes! I'm going to ask her to the concert at the Circle Club on Friday."

The calmness that Ben felt before had now turned to a raging madness. *How dare he try and take her away?* It was so difficult to keep his eyebrows from scrunching up into wrinkles.

"Ryan ... shouldn't you be thinking more about how *well* we do at the club ... not who will be there? I thought we had practice tonight, man," Ben said, crossing his arms.

"Tuh!" Ryan made a sound on the roof of his mouth. "Come on dude, you don't really think one night will make a difference. Besides, I know my stuff."

"Yeah, but we can't practice without you!" Ben was losing his cool. "You're the beat ... you're the rhythm! How are we supposed to have any tempo?"

Ryan's smile was now gone. "Hey, chill out man. I'm not going anywhere, it's just one date."

Emily E. Shipp

"One date? Look what happened to Mark! He almost never came to practice because he was always with Marsha, and now it's going to happen to you, too. The only reason he's still in the band is because he dumped her!"

"So you're saying," Ryan started, putting one hand on his hip, "that I can't be in the band with a girlfriend, too?"

Girlfriend. Clem. The words bubbled inside Ben's bloodstream until the organs were about to burst.

"You know what? Just forget it!" Ben yelled, turning away.

Ryan was stunned for a minute, then he ran after Ben and clutched his wrist. "Ben!" Ryan yelled. "What's your deal? You're going all whack on me because I'm going out with Clem for one night. What's the biggie?"

"I said forget it!"

There were moments and moments of nothing. Ben, who was angrily staring at the confused Ryan, was full of emotion in the now empty hallway. But before Ryan could say anything, Ben jerked his arm away with a scowl.

"You're my best friend, and you don't even get it."

The sad thing was, when he was walking away, he knew he was walking away from one of the best friendships he had ever had.

~

She waited for him in jeans and a red, long-sleeved shirt with the word "cutie" spread across the top, its letters embroidered with silver sequins. Her hair was up in a smooth ponytail, her makeup was carefully applied, and she had just slid on her sparkling white tennis shoes—the ones she had bought with Scarlett, but hadn't worn yet. Her jean jacket made the outfit. She smiled as she walked out of the house. She was proud of herself. She was looking very American, if she did say so herself.

The Lopsided Miracle

She had invited Jodie to wait with her for Ryan to come, but Jodie had gotten quiet and said she had homework to finish, but thanked her anyway.

The scary thing is, Clem thought, shivering in her jacket, *that Jodie might like the one person who likes me here.*

Clem didn't want one of her only friends to think she was the villain in her crush situation, but guiltily she thought, *What about me? What if I like him? Aren't I entitled to like him, too?*

The whole situation was so confusing.

Just as she was thinking about this, she saw a dark blue Mercedes Benz drive around the corner and into the driveway. Ryan opened the door and jumped out, coming around to the other side and opening the door for her. Clem walked up to him with a lopsided smile on her face.

"Wow," she said.

"You first, cutie," said Ryan, looking down at her shirt.

Clem giggled and sat down in the car. The interior smelled new. "Is this new?" she asked as he sat down inside, too. Clem couldn't help but notice that he looked very nice.

"Well," he said, blushing and desperately trying to hide it, "actually, it's a rental."

Clem laughed. "Well, if it makes you feel any better, it looks great." Ryan didn't say anything, but Clem hated silence, so she struck up another topic. "So where are we going?"

He seemed to be extremely relieved that Clem had asked him this. "Uh ... I was thinking just a burger or something."

"You got *this* car for a burger?" Clem asked, raising an eyebrow, but keeping her grin. He looked a little offended again. "Well," Clem quickly said, "I meant ... that's a great idea. I love it!"

He smiled again, backing the car out of the driveway. "Well, I *think* I can tell when a girl is disappointed." Clem gave a forced laugh. Actually, she hadn't been disappointed. A burger had sounded fine.

Emily E. Shipp

"So," Ryan continued, "I have a place that would be great for you. I hope you're hungry."

Ryan drove down the road and, after a few moments of silence, decided to show off a little. He sped up the car about ten marks above the speed limit and cruised down the road like there was no tomorrow.

Unfortunate as it was to spoil Ryan's fun, Clem wanted to live to see the next day. "Ryan, stop speeding. There are cop cars everywhere."

"Don't worry, I know what I'm doing." He sped up five more marks.

"Ryan ..."

"Clem, don't worry about it! I've done this a million times before."

"Ryan!"

Ryan jerked his head forward, and Clem hurriedly reached over in her seat to help spin the wheel to the left so that they veered off the wrong one-way road Ryan had accidentally turned on to.

"*Ahhh*!" Ryan screamed loudly. "My car!" The new car bumped down into a ditch and was, unfortunately or fortunately (depending on how you look at it), stopped by a huge mud puddle that splashed all over the front end of the automobile.

They both sat in a stunned silence, frozen in their positions for a moment or two, before all of a sudden Clem started laughing.

"Ha*ha*!" She laughed a big, hearty, relieved laugh. "Oh my *gosh* R-Ryan! Did you see the *look* on your *face* when we went into the ... the ..." She was laughing so hard that her face was red and her words came out stuttered.

Ryan wasn't laughing at all, though. "Clem!" he yelled. She looked over at his face and was immediately put out of glee. He was angry. "This is not funny! This car cost me a lot of money, and now I am not even going to be able to return it to the dealership!" He banged his head on the steering wheel. "Not to mention this date is ruined," he added quietly.

Clem had wondered why he was so angry, but as soon as he mumbled the last words, she smiled slightly. "Hey, come on! It's not ruined! You just think it is."

Ryan didn't seem to be encouraged by this. "No. No, Clem, it's ruined! The car ... we can't push it out without looking like we ran into a pile of cow crap, and we can't go to *Le Mount* ..."

"*Le Mount*? Where's that?" Clem asked, interrupting him.

He sighed. "It's a really nice place where I made reservations."

Wow, Clem thought, *he looks really disappointed. I've got to do something.*

"Well," she started, smiling slyly, "I don't know much about you Canadians, but we Americans do first dates a little ... differently."

Ryan laughed. "You know, I bet my producers are probably wondering where I am," he said, taking a sip of his chocolate milkshake.

"What do you mean, producers?" Clem asked, taking a bite of her burger. Her once-clean hair was now muddy and in a messy ponytail.

"Well, you know, I'm an actor. My life is an open book. I bet the guy who made the reservations for me told on me."

Clem nodded, using her pinky to shove a piece of lettuce back in her mouth. "Right," she said with a full mouth.

Ryan laughed again. His attitude had changed completely since the accident with the car. Clem had finally made him get out of the car and help her push the car out of the mud.

"Stand on the side of the road! People will recognize you and help us!" Clem had said.

"No way," Ryan had replied. "All those girls coming up to me and giving death threats to you? Don't think so." They had gotten covered with mud while trying to get the car out of the ditch, but after about a half

Emily E. Shipp

hour of pushing and shoving and restarting the engine about a trillion times, the car was back on the road.

At that point, Ryan was mad about their muddy attire for dinner, but Clem assured him that where they were going, their attire wouldn't matter at all.

She directed him to a burger place she had seen along the way, a little place that most people would just look right over. The food was very good, though, and no one was there except the staff.

"You know," Ryan snapped her back into the present, "we've had a pretty good time together."

"Yeah," Clem said, smiling, "Considering what we went through, it was pretty good."

"Will you go out with me this Friday?" Ryan asked her so fast, Clem wasn't even sure she had heard him right.

She shook her head. "What?" she asked, blinking.

Ryan seemed more confident now. "Will you go out with me, again, this Friday? I'm playing at the Circle Club, and I ..."

"Oh," Clem interrupted him, trying desperately to think of some excuse to not go besides being away from Ben—but he wouldn't understand that. "Um, I don't know. There will be ... a lot of people there ... and I don't know if I am ready for ..." *Think, THINK!* A little voice screamed inside Clem's head. She blurted out the first thing that came to her mind, "People might think of us as a ... couple! And, well, I don't think I'm ready for that." *Smooth*, she thought to herself.

Ryan put on his puppy-dog look again. "But, this is my first gig, and I wanted you to be there." *Oh, please.* He looked down at the table and slouched. He didn't look cute. He looked pitiful. What would he think of her if she didn't say yes?

This is a TV star, hun! Scarlett's voice popped into her head all of a sudden. *Go for the gold! Go out with him!*

She gulped, "Well ..." *Why am I doing this to myself?* "Okay."

The Lopsided Miracle

    Ryan's head jerked up and a large smile spread across his face. "Okay!" he said, taking a sip of milkshake. Clem sighed. She knew she would have to confront Ben there, as well as all of the fans that would be in his face. But the strange thing was that she knew the same thing, fans galore, would happen to Ryan, too.
    So why don't I ... care?

CHAPTER EIGHTEEN

The place was completely packed!

Ben couldn't help cracking a smile. This was going to rock!

Well, he thought, his smile dimming, *except that Clem isn't going to be here.*

It was Friday night. Three's No Crowd was all decked out in jazzy gear and sunglasses for the light. There were mostly girls there, who were looking all around the crowded area to find the celebrities, but there were also a few unhappy boyfriends that looked miffed to be there. The band had agreed to an autograph signing at the end of the performance. Ben couldn't help but think of how his hand would hurt after tonight.

Ben closed the door, hoping no one had seen him, and walked over to Mark, who was practicing a bit on his keyboard in the big auditorium that they had auditioned in.

"Where's Ryan?" Mark asked as soon as Ben closed the door again.

"He's not out there," Ben said, gulping. He was getting worried about Ryan. They had to start in ten minutes, and he wasn't there yet.

"What?" Mark was as worried as Ben was. "Oh great. What are we going to do if he doesn't show up?" Mark rubbed his temples. He looked nervous.

"Don't worry about it. In the worst-case scenario, we'll have to …"Ben didn't have to finish his sentence because there was a knock at the door.

"Yo!" A familiar voice called through. Ben sighed a sigh of relief and opened the door. He saw a body in a long, black coat and a blue baseball cap. His head was down until the door clicked open. "Get me

Emily E. Shipp

in! I think a few girls noticed my face," he said. He rushed in and Ben closed the door.

"What took you so long? I was about to hire another percussionist!" Mark said loudly.

"Hush!" Ryan said. Then, taking off his coat, he smiled smugly. "But I have a good excuse. I was picking up my date."

Ben's heart started beating faster.

"I didn't know you dated!" Mark said, kidding around, but then seriously he said, "Who?"

Ryan grinned, and without hesitation said, "Clem."

Ben widened his eyes—but only for a minute. He decided not to say anything, but guiltily, he wished he could wring his best friend's neck. *Peachy*, he thought sarcastically. But then, as he watched Ryan take out his drumsticks and pretend to rock on imaginary drums, Ben smiled.

But at least now she's here, he thought. The door opened suddenly and all three turned their heads sharply to see if they would have to defend themselves as they went onstage. It was Mr. Pitching. He was wearing a suit and looked even more nervous than the band.

"All right," he started, "this is it." He dabbed his forehead with a white cloth. Ben, Ryan and Mark stood up, waiting for him to finish. "You," he said, pointing a finger towards Ryan. "Your drums are already outside.

"Do you want me to take the keyboard out for you?" Mark nodded. Mr. Pitching snapped his fingers and almost immediately the two guards that had saved them the last time came in, and one took up the keyboard. He left and came back quickly, after Mr. Pitching explained that he was going to give the band an introduction, and then they would be allowed to come out with the two guards. The three boys nodded. Mr. Pitching took a huge, shaky breath and then walked out, his black shoes clicking on the tile. The door closed behind him.

The Lopsided Miracle

Of course, Ben, Ryan, and Mark were way too curious about how they would be introduced and opened the door slightly so they could look out. Ben watched excitedly as the audience went from chatting and laughing to applause as Mr. Pitching came up on stage. He cleared his throat into the microphone. The applause went down.

"Thank you, thank you," he said in a gruff tone. "Well, I would just like to welcome you and thank you all for coming to the Circle Club tonight on this ... special night." Applause. "Yes, thank you. I would just like to say, before we bring out our special guests, please do not crowd them. We will have an autograph signing after the performance. If you would like to stay until then, you are more than welcome to." Applause. "So," he said. All the girls knew what this meant, so they started giggling and fixing their hair. "Without further ado, I would like to present, for their first musical performance ever ... Three's No Crowd!"

Everyone screamed and clapped. Ben was frozen. Could this really be happening?

"Ben! *Go!*" Mark yelled. Ben shook his head and pushed open the door. One of the guards stood in front of him and the other one stood behind Mark and Ryan, as they walked in a single file to the steps leading to the stage. All the screeching fans tried to get close to them, but the guards gave them stern looks, and everyone stayed away.

The band stepped up onto the stage, and Ben was relieved that they had decided to wear sunglasses. The florescent lighting was positively blinding.

Then there he was. Standing smack dab in the middle of the stage, his sunglasses on and a nervous smile on his face. He thought to himself that he had never been this nervous before, ever. But maybe that was also because he had never tried to impress someone with his music before, either. He looked out among the crowd; it seemed so big from up there. He felt as though he was on top of the world.

But then she came out of nowhere. With her hair as straight as a stick, but lying softly on her shoulders, she looked so familiar. And she

Emily E. Shipp

was wearing a simple white shirt and jeans. While everyone else was decked out, she looked the most perfect of them all.

He smiled at her, but she wasn't smiling back. Slipping on his guitar, he spoke into the microphone. "Hey," he said. Everyone screamed. He gave a small laugh. "Thanks for coming, it, um, it really means a lot to us." All the girls sighed. "But right now I want to introduce the band. We met on the show *The Truth Told by Me*, and when we found our love for music, we formed a band, and this is where we are now."

"Ahhhhh!" Someone started the next round of cheering. Ben could tell who it was by the annoyingly high-pitched tone. He looked out and saw Fiona Whitewaters standing next to her clique and clapping wildly. Ben was almost embarrassed by her.

"So let me introduce everyone before we start," he said. He swept his arm over to Mark's direction. "Everyone, this is Mark Olshire, the master of the keyboard!" Mark did a stunning routine on the keyboard that sent the whole crowd whistling and clapping.

"This," Ben said, breaking the applause, "is the second member of the band—our percussionist and best friend, Ryan Matthews!" The crowd also clapped at Ryan's number. Then Ben looked back to the crowd for his first debut. "And I'm the guitarist— Ben Clavis!" Every girl in the entire room (except one in particular) screamed so loudly, Ben was actually sent backwards, but only a tiny bit. He played a jazzy guitar part, and then smiled and laughed, looking at Mark and Ryan. Everyone was thrilled.

"Okay," he said. "Let's get started." He signaled the number three on his fingers and then the other two nodded. Ryan started, tapping gently on the drums.

"One! Two! One, two, three, *four*!"

The performance started with a bang, and the songs in between were sweet, too. Most people just stared during the first couple of songs,

The Lopsided Miracle

but then some people started dancing while others headed to the food stand. But some kept staring. Fiona made a show of dancing (in a way she thought was sexy) right up front. Ben wasn't paying attention to her, though. In fact, he rarely took his eyes off Clem the whole time. He found her actions very unusual, though. The way she just stood there the whole time, it was as if she were made of plastic and her eyes would not move unless someone put his fingers on them and moved them for her. If Ben didn't know any better, he would say that she was trying to win a staring contest with him. The only motion she ever made was a slight cocking of her head, as if to say, "Who are you?"

Another strange thing that occurred throughout the performance was that whenever Ben held up his fingers to signal that he wanted to play the slow song he had written for Clem, Ryan shook his head vigorously. Ben tried and tried to start it, but Ryan would always move into another song, and Mark would follow.

Finally, Mr. Pitching came up and told them they could have their break. The band members sighed and were taken off by the guards. They headed towards the back room again, but before they closed the door, Ryan whispered something to one of the guards. He nodded. Then he grunted and closed the door.

"I'm starving!" Mark said. "I hope they have good food at this joint."

"Really," Ben said. He looked over at Ryan from the corner of his eye and saw that he looked about ready to burst. "Ryan, what's up? You look like you have a bomb up your pants." Ryan grinned as the door opened.

Ben turned around and saw Jodie come in. She was wearing her red wig that she wore when she didn't want to be noticed. She took it off and shook her hair around her.

"Hey!" she said. She walked over to Ryan and put her arms around his waist. Ryan let her.

Emily E. Shipp

Ben's mouth dropped to the floor. What was going on? "You freak! How could you do this to Clem?" he asked, outraged.

Ryan smiled. So did Jodie. "Ben," Ryan said, "I'm not a player like that. I'm not blind either."

Ben was lost. He felt like everyone knew something he didn't.

"Ben, it was totally obvious. Everyone *except* Clem knows ... you like her."

Ben's heart stopped. So what was going on?

"But ... I thought you were her date! I thought you went out with her and liked her and everything!" Ben said.

"Well, I did!" Ryan said, taking Jodie's arms off of him. "But that was only until I saw that you liked her way more than I ever could. So I asked her out to get her to come here, so *you* could ask her out. I didn't tell her during the date, but I told her today and she knows now. She said she used to like you, but after you hurt her, she had mixed feelings. She was even going to give up her part as Cinderella because of you! Now that I've told her about... you ..." He paused. "Well, maybe she's willing to give you a second chance."

Ben was stunned. He had mixed feelings, too. He was grateful and angry and confused all at the same time.

"You mean, you asked her out to help *me* and ... *all* that time you were acting?"

Ryan shrugged. "Hey, man. That's my job."

Ben didn't know what to do, but at the same time he did. Shakily, he asked, "What about you?"

Ryan grinned and looked back at Jodie. "I'm fine," he said.

~

Clem was having the strangest night of her life. Ryan's words, his plan, everything he said about Ben had been so surreal. But now she was here, at the Circle Club, watching her old crush sing almost

The Lopsided Miracle

beautifully out into the audience—into Clem. Not once had he taken his eyes off of her, and not once had she tried to glance away.

Now, she was crowded back into a huddle of people since the band had come back on stage. There he was. Scanning the crowd for her again, and when he found her, he spoke into the microphone. "Hey, everyone, we're back." Ben and the band were greeted with loud applause, but Ben hardly noticed. His eyes were trained on Clem again. "I would like to call up someone really ... um, really special to the stage." There was a long pause, every girl hoping it was going to be herself called up. "Clem Greenly, can you come up?"

There was polite applause, but even that was just confused. Who was this girl? And the people who did know her were so jealous that they were green. Fiona looked as though she would faint again.

Clem passed everyone, feeling incredibly confident. She didn't know what was going to happen, but she had a feeling it was good. When she was up on the stage, everything stopped. It felt as though time was frozen, and Ben and Clem were the only ones moving. Clem looked up into his eyes.

"Clem," he said. It echoed through the microphone even though he didn't mean for it to. "I'm ... sorry." Clem opened her mouth to say something, but Ben stopped her. "No, let me finish," he started. He took a deep breath and closed his eyes, then opened them again. "I'm sorry. When ... when you first arrived here, I thought ... well, I thought my whole life was going to be ruined. I thought you would be ... a lot less than you really are. It was that day the paper came out that I lost it. I didn't know what to do, so I took everything out on you, which was probably the biggest mistake of my life. Clem, I'm really sorry, and ... I hope you accept my apology."

Clem's eyes welled up with tears and before she could stop herself, she leaned in to give him a kiss that sent the crowd roaring and

Emily E. Shipp

whistling (and Fiona fainting),but the best part about it was that both of them knew it would be the first kiss of many.

Neither of them would have traded that for anything.

PART THREE

CHAPTER NINETEEN

Dear Diary,
    I haven't written in a while, and for that I am sorry, but I have had a lot going on! The Valentine's Day dance has passed and it was great! Ryan, Jodie, Katherine, Joel (remember the Swedish exchange student?), Ben, and I all went on a triple date out to eat and then danced the night away!
    And remember the play, Cinderella? Well, Fiona made a great stepmother! She even forgot one of her lines, and lucky for her, I saved her. As for the kiss at the end, I had no trouble mastering that! Ben is really a great guy, now that I have been given the chance to get to know him better—and I still love his show!
    Speaking of the show, as a gift from Ben and the rest of the staff, I was given a role to play in an episode! I play—what else?—an exchange student! It was so much fun, and at the end, I got a photo of the cast signed by everyone (even the makeup artists!) and later, I received a five-page photo album of pictures from the set—including one of Jodie and me, one of Ben and me, and even one of me in the director's chair!
    School has been going well, too. Fiona stays out of my way now, and whenever she sees Ben with me, I always think she will faint again (fainting Fiona—how does that sound?) But that's okay, because he never liked her anyway.
    But the greatest thing about being in Canada is the experience I have had with Ben. We go to different places and do tons of different things—and Scarlett is very jealous! I am just wondering how we will stay in touch when I have to leave again to go back to South Carolina.

Emily E. Shipp
Ben said he doesn't want to think about it, and I don't really, either. We've had too much of a wonderful time to think about it ending yet.

One thing is for sure—everything that has happened to me has been a miracle. I mean how many girls get to have a TV star boyfriend? I know, not many, but considering all the strange and hurtful things that have occurred along the way, it definitely has been a little lopsided. Yet, lopsided miracle or not, it doesn't matter.

It is still a miracle.

ABOUT THE AUTHOR

Emily E. Shipp, now living in South Carolina after living in Michigan and Tennessee, has been writing for as long as she can remember. *"The Lopsided Miracle"* is her very first published novel, and she hopes to create many more throughout her lifetime. She thanks all of her friends and family for all her success. She also wants to thank the celebrities she observed to help create bits and pieces of the characters in the story.

She one day hopes to be on "Oprah", be in a movie, and go to Paris.